Full
CIRCLE

RICHARD ELLIS SHAW

outskirts
press

Outskirts Press, Inc.
http://www.outskirtspress.com

ISBN: 978-1-9772-0462-2

Outskirts Press and the "OP" logo are trademarks belonging to Outskirts Press, Inc.

PRINTED IN THE UNITED STATES OF AMERICA

I would like to thank my Outskirts Press, author Rep Deni, for her patience and great advice. I would like to thank my editor for her keen eyes and expertise. I would also like to thank Brenda, for believing in me. Special thanks to Willie and Mac for encuraging me to keep going. To my friends' thanks for the support and encouragement.

OTHER BOOKS WRITTEN BY RICHARD ELLIS SHAW

THE HEART OF A POET

Poetry is the creation of an image, an emotion or even a picture in the mind of the reader. The power of one word is truly tested within the lines of a poem. My poems tell a story.

A TAPESTRY: OF LIFE'S JOURNEYS

This is a book of ten short stories.

THE GIFT – love letters and a doll's cradle

MISSING SUMMER- treasure-college graduation-small town relationships

AUTHOR'S CHARACTER- blank pages-character's revenge

REBIRTH- finally figuring out who she is

THE PHOTOGRAPHER-double dog dare-strange camera-and a photographer

SUSIE'S DINER-small town- characters life changing

CHANCE ENCOUNTER-stepping outside her comfort zone

INTERLOPER-noises and lights in an abandoned farmhouse

SNOW DAY-no school-best day ever

DUSTY BOOK EMPORIUM-unexplained journey into a bookstore-maybe

PROLOGUE

Pike and his old college roommate, Tony sat back in their Adirondack chairs watching the sun slide down the far horizon, eventually slipping into the Atlantic Ocean. Tony held up his beer toward Pike,

"Did you ever think about how many sunsets we have watched together?" Tony's words had a slow rhythm to them.

"Probably more sunsets than sunrises."

"Tony, do you remember the first time we came down to your parent's cottage?"

Pike turned to Tony,

"Yes, it was our junior year in college, Maggie, and Julie, you and I. It was the first time the girls visited Pelican Island and experienced the Atlantic Ocean."

"That was a wonderful time. Sun, beach, girls, and spring break. Remember sitting around a fire on the beach with a salt-drenched breeze off the ocean, the sparks from the fire dancing in the sky."

"I also remember how difficult it was to go back to campus at the end of the break."

"Yeah, I always looked forward to seeing you, sitting on the beach around a fire, accompanied by the sound of waves slapping the beach. Telling stories. For just a moment forgetting we are not the same innocent kids we were when we met at college."

"I know you've told me about what broke you and Maggie up many years ago. Then you eventually got back together. Never mentioned that break-up since. Whatever happened to the two of you?"

"That was a long time ago." Pike's eyes shifted from Tony to the fire. Pike tossed another log on, sat back as a shower of sparks raced toward the black, starless sky.

Pike shifted in his chair, opened another bottle of beer, took a long drag, closed his eyes, then began to speak. "Let me start from the beginning.

1

1980

The day, one of those perfect autumn days, that sometimes occurs in Chicago. Yellow leaves of an ancient hickory tree danced in the flickering rays of the morning sun in the center of Bolton College Commons. Leaves were at their peak, each tree having exchanged its green summer shawl for a vibrant, flamboyant fall cloak. The red leaves of two Norwegian Maples stood in sharp contrast to the still green grasses of the past summer. Early fall pulled students out of their dorm rooms. They walked around, gathering in small groups, enjoying the afternoon sun on the Commons, surrounded by dorms and classrooms. The stone-faced chapel stood regally at the east corner of the Commons.

Couples moved a little closer to each other as a breeze from the north drifted across campus. Upperclassmen returning to campus for the fall rekindled romances that lay dormant over the summer.

Carter Gym, the oldest building on campus, stood alone, facing the center of the Commons. The well-worn stone steps led up to the whitewashed steel doors with spots of rust showing its age. As was the tradition, as a gift to the freshman class, the senior class handled decorating the gym for homecoming dance. The faded yellow bricks lining the walls of the gym transformed into an autumn motif as promised by the seniors.

Friday finally arrived; the night clear and crisp as Pike and Tony walked across campus. Music emanating from the gym slipped out of the open front door and spread its steady beat across the small campus. Students huddling around the Commons area, gathered their jackets, and moved toward the gym, some in pairs, others in small groups. A mixture of students wore shorts and sweatshirts while others wore jeans and T-shirts. Some girls dressed in jeans while others shivered in short skirts.

Pike and Tony strolled into the dance. Standing together inside the old gym, they let their eyes wander across the floor, watching the girls dancing and many of the guys standing in small groups watching.

The music came from a three-piece band playing on stage. The floor filled with students, each moving to their own interpretation of the music. Pike and Tony soon separated. Pike looked across the gym and caught sight of a brown-haired girl with a smile that made him catch his breath. She looked directly at him, or at least that was what he thought. He stood watching her move around the room, occasionally glancing in Pike's direction. For a moment, everything in the gym stopped, the music faded into the background, and the other students seemed frozen in space.

She circled around the dance floor, walking in front of Pike two or three times. The third time, he touched her arm "Want to dance? I'm not a good dancer, want to take a chance?" Pike's voice trailed off as she turned to face him.

"I'll take a chance." She looked directly into his eyes, smiled, strolled into a swarm of bodies moving in all different directions. Pike followed, trying to remember the last time he tried to dance. At the end of the dance she stood looking at him as the music stopped.

"My name is Pike." A long hesitation. She smiled and looked up at him.

"My name is Margaret, but everyone calls me Maggie." She smiled, "You were right." Pike glanced up. "You're not a very good dancer – but you do have a great smile."

"Want to try again?" Pike smiled.

The music started again, Pike and Maggie blended in with the other dancers. When the music changed to a slow dance, Pike was grateful. He took Maggie's hand, and led her into an open spot on the floor. Maggie looked up at Pike "Maybe there is hope for you after all." They both laughed.

The gym grew hot with so many people moving around and no windows to let the outside in.

"You want to get out of here for some fresh air?"

She seemed to be thinking about it.

"Does that line really work?"

Pike started to say something, then realized she was teasing him.

Yes," she said, beginning to walk toward the door. As they stepped outside, the cool air brushed against their faces. Slowly they walked down the steps to the sidewalk, and around the Commons. Pike listened as Maggie talked about her roommate, Jane. "She was the first person I met here at college. We're both from the Midwest. Hey, where are you from, are you from around here?"

"A small town in New England. First time in the Midwest. My roommate, Tony, is from New Jersey. He and I seem to get along well."

Conversation seemed to flow easily between Pike and Maggie as they walked around the inner circle of the campus.

Pike was the first to break the silence. "You said you were from the Midwest, somewhere close to here?" Where are you from?" She stopped walking, turned to face him, and spoke softly. "I live on campus, but I am from a small town about a hundred miles from here."

Pike hesitated. "Would you like some hot Chocolate in the student union?"

"Sounds good."

Pike and Maggie walked toward the student union each lost in their own thoughts. The union was empty, most students attending the dance in the gym. Armed with a cup of hot chocolate each, they found a small round table and two chairs. Holding her mug with both hands, Maggie blew across the top of the cup as the steam circled above the cup. She swirled the remains of her chocolate around in her cup and waited for Pike to speak.

Conversation became easy as Maggie and Pike learned about each other. Pike sipped his drink. "Tomorrow's supposed to be a day like today. There's a football game—first game of the season. But we don't have a very good team."

Maggie looked over the rim of her mug and brushed her hair back behind her left ear as she did when she was nervous. "Okay? Guess I'll see you at the game."

As students began appearing, Maggie and Pike realized the dance was over. When they arrived at the front steps of the old stone chapel at the western corner of the campus, they stopped and looked into each other's eyes and for a moment felt at peace.

The words that had so freely woven them together through-out the night got stuck in their throats. Hesitantly Pike leaned over and tenderly kissed Maggie and was surprised when she gently returned his kiss. A tightness shot down Pike's chest and rested somewhere near his heart; it took a moment to catch his breath. Later when they would speak of this first kiss, they each knew that it changed their lives.

As Maggie and Pike stood looking at the campus from the steps to Maggie's dorm, emotions and images flooded his mind. He wondered how he'd been pulled so deeply into the brown eyes of the girl standing next to him.

Tony came walking up with a dark-haired girl. She turned out to be Maggie's best friend, Julie. Maggie smiled at her friend, and turned to Tony. "We're going to the football game tomorrow. Why don't you guys come too?" Julie's eyes seemed to darken as she stared back at Maggie. It seemed for a moment as if neither Tony nor Julie were excited about the prospect.

Tony started to make his excuse for not being able to make it when Julie turned to Maggie and said,

"We would love to go." Tony felt trapped and looked at his friend for help. One look at Pike and he knew that it was a lost cause. Strangely he hoped Julie would suddenly change her mind, but she locked eyes on him and Tony knew that there was no way out.

"Yes, it sounds like fun," Tony said with all the emotion he could summon. Later he knew Pike would be in his debt. Tony had to take Julie to the game on Saturday.

Later as Tony and Pike walked back to their dorm, Tony asked,

"Where did you disappear to during the dance? I looked for you." Pike just smiled and said he had walked the girl named Maggie back to her dorm.

Saturday morning arrived with the sun breaking through the blinds in their dorm room. Pike turned over and hugged his pillow. He opened his eyes and looked over at the clock. It was 8:00 a.m. Reaching for his pillow, he threw it across the room, hitting Tony. The snoring stopped, and Tony propped himself up on one elbow.

"You owe me," Tony's voice was still gravelly from sleep.

"I know, I know, Julie seems like a nice girl. But what's the problem?"

"She asks too many questions; she has an opinion about everything. I'll go to the game, but you owe me."

Tony and Pike walked across the Commons to the student union and made their way into the cafeteria for breakfast. As they entered the dining area Maggie waved.

Tony looked at Julie and waved. Pike sipped his coffee and watched Maggie and Julie as they finished their breakfast.

The game started at noon. Julie turned and looked at Maggie "You know you owe me. I'm only going because you want to go with Pike. What kind of a name is Pike anyway?"

The Bolton Chargers once again lived up to their reputation. The game ended in another loss: 21-0.

As does time in college and college romances, the next four years flew by. Maggie and Pike became inseparable as they attended classes together, shared meals together. They strolled around campus or spent time with her family on the weekends in the beginning and then, as the years passed, Pike would almost become a part of her family. The relationship was one that seemed to help both enliven them and allow them to evolve into two strong people.

2

COLLEGE YEARS

Pike awoke early the day after the final formal dance in the student union; there were so many emotions and thoughts racing around in his head. Getting up, he walked to the window, and peered out at the trees in the commons. Spring was showing her best colors with the help of the morning sun, just beginning to pop up over the horizon.

Pike glanced around the room that had been his during his senior year. There was a knock at the door and there Maggie stood with a coffee in each hand. Pike ran his fingers through his hair, leaned over and kissed her.

Maggie and Pike walked to the student union and found a seat with Tony and Julie.

"Good morning, Julie," Maggie said. Tony was eating a stack of pancakes, some scrambled eggs, and a couple of sausage links. Julie set down some fruit and her large coffee, black. Pike wondered how Tony could eat all that food so early in the morning and never gained a pound.

Pike set his mug down and smiled at his friends. Pike watched Tony and Julie tease each other. They seemed to have a private conversation going on between them without a word being spoken. Pike glanced at his watch, ten minutes till Russian History class. Maggie lifted her cup and winked at him.

"Did you prepare your presentation for today?" Maggie asked. She already knew the answer.

"Oh, Professor Wilson won't call on me today, I'll work on it tonight, no problem," Pike said.

Tony and Julie laughed; Pike would never change.

Professor Wilson walked up to the podium and cleared his throat, which signaled students he was about to speak. The auditorium fell silent as he opened his notebook, turned on the overhead projector, and began his lecture. Pike sat back in his seat confident that the professor would not get to him today. Opening his notebook, he began to write notes from the lecture.

There were two other students scheduled to also give their presentations. As the other two students completed their presentations, the clock on the wall indicated that there was only ten minutes left in class.

The professor looked at his watch and then at Pike. He was sure that Pike was not ready to present, so he decided to call his bluff.

"Pike, would you care to present for us today?" As soon as the words left his mouth, he realized that he had given Pike a way out.

Pike stood up with what seemed like a presentation in his hands.

"I would be glad to present today; however, due to the depth of my research it would take me more than the ten minutes left in class. I know that some of the other students have a class after this and might be late if I were to take the time to present today."

"Well, would the next class work for you?" the professor asked, his voice dripping with sarcasm.

The students walked out of class heading for their next class or to the student union. Pike walked to the union to meet Maggie after her class.

"Well, how did your presentation go?"

"The professor ran out of time, I must present next week." Pike said with a smile.

"I know this is a foolish question, but did you have your presentation ready for class?"

Pike looked at her and smiled.

"Pike, graduation is only a month away you need a decent grade in that course." As she spoke, she reached out and put her hands over his.

Tony and Julie came in holding hands and seemed to be excited about something. Tony sat down across from Pike in a booth.

"Ok, Tony, spill it what is going on?" Pike knew his friend long enough to know when he was hiding something.

"My parents are going on a trip during spring break, which means the cottage will be empty. Julie and I are going; how about you guys?"

Pike and Maggie looked at each other and Pike said

"We will have to talk about it, but it sounds like a fantastic way to end our senior year."

Tony looked at his watch, next class was starting in an hour and he was hungry. Tony and Julie got up and headed for the cafeteria.

"Maggie, think you can get away?" Maggie leaned forward and said, "I would love to, but I'm not sure what my parents are doing that week if they expect me to be home."

Maggie hesitated. "Pelican Island is such a unique place, every time we've gone there, it's been great.

"Remember our first time...?" Pike smiled as he thought about their first time sleeping together. She smiled as she whispered, "We were so nervous."

Maggie and Pike met later to study in the library. Pike was typing an essay for his English class. Maggie watched him; he seemed lost in his writing, as if no one else existed. He was so different when working on his writing rather than courses in his history major. Writing was not a chore; Maggie could see it in his eyes.

"Maggie, may I read something to you or can you read this page?" Maggie had a feeling that he would soon find that writing was much more important than his history classes.

Maggie decided she would go to Pelican Island with Pike, Tony, and Julie for spring break. She'd told her parents she and Julie were going to go to Julie's house in Tennessee for a week.

Pike finally gave his presentation in Russian History and got an

A. He researched and drafted the paper for the presentation in two nights. Maggie smiled. She was so different than Pike. She planned everything, set a schedule, and had every assignment finished a week before it was due. Planning and organization were part of her personality. Pike on the other hand seemed to do everything at the last minute. However, he always did well. They each wished they could be a little more like the other.

Early Saturday morning after the semester ended the four friends piled into Tony's GTO and headed for Pelican Island. The trip filled them with anticipation and shared memories of the other trips to Pelican Island. After navigating for four hours, Pike and Maggie switched positions and got into the back of the GTO. Soon Tony glanced in his rearview mirror. Maggie was asleep with her head on Pike's shoulder and Pike was asleep leaning against the side of the car door. Julie took a picture to add to their photo album.

3

SENIOR SPRING BREAK

Pelican Island

The small faded white cottage sat behind a sand dune covered with tan grasses waving in the ocean breeze. The front porch faced the sea beyond the sand dunes. Two white rockers built by Tony's grandfather sat on either side of the screen door leading into the cottage.

Julie and Maggie stepped out of the back of the GTO, took off their sandals, and let their feet warm up in the pure white sand. While the girls walked toward the porch, Tony and Pike carried suitcases from the car to the cottage.

Stepping into the living room of the cottage, the friends were assaulted with the smell of dampness and dust. Opening windows allowed the salt air from the ocean to sweep out the stale odors.

Tony and Julie took their suitcases to the bedroom off the living room. Pike took Maggie's hand and walked into the back bedroom, falling on the bed as if exhausted.

"On no you don't! We're going to go to the beach," Maggie said, standing at the foot of the bed, both hands on her hips. Pike smiled, he knew he was not going to win this maneuver.

After a quick change of clothes, the two couples ran toward the beach and the sound of waves lapping the shore. Pike kept on running, throwing himself into an oncoming wave. He disappeared beneath the waves only to pop up about ten feet further out. As he floated on his back the warmth of the water soothed him.

"Come on! The water is great." The others soon followed. After a refreshing swim, they retired to the beach, drying under the mid-morning sun. Tony asked about lunch.

Tony and Pike agreed to go grocery shopping and the girls agreed to fix lunch but wanted to go to Slippery Rock Bar that evening for the best seafood in town. Pike and Tony returned with the groceries and found an empty house. A note on the refrigerator solved the mystery.

Maggie and Julie walked along the beach looking for starfish and sand dollars. The two had been friends from the first day they were roommates their freshman year. Over the years they'd shared their feelings about their relationships with Pike and Tony.

"Can I tell you a secret?" Julie's eyes exploded with excitement. Maggie stopped and turned to her friend.

"What's up?" Maggie had a feeling she already knew. Tony and Julie had been spending increasingly more time together this year.

"Tony bought me a ring, but I'm not supposed to know about it. I accidently found it. I was picking up his pants off the floor, when I stayed over last week."

Maggie hugged her friend... "How do you feel about it?" Maggie's voice was just above a murmur.

"I don't know, so many feelings racing around inside of me. I know I love him, but I'm only twenty-three years old." Julie's voice suddenly sounded slightly pensive.

Maggie could sympathize with her friend. She and Pike had been talking about the future after college.

"We've talked about finding a place to live also," said Maggie. "I don't know how I feel. I do love him..." It was the first time she'd said it to someone else. Both women stopped walking and stood gazing at the endless ocean that seemed to stretch out in front of them forever.

"Maybe that's why it's so scary... Forever," Maggie blurted out as she bent down to pick up a sand dollar. Brushing it off, she put it in her pocket.

They started walking back to the cottage. In the distance two figures were waving their hands in the air. Waving back, they realized it was Tony and Pike. Maggie stopped walking,

"I don't think our conversation is over," Maggie whispered to Julie.

Sitting on the beach after dinner, they watched the sun drop slowly into the sea. Pike built a fire with driftwood he found on the beach. The flames reached skyward and sparks danced on the sea breezes.

Conversation focused on finals coming up and what to do after college. Maggie already had a job lined up. She would be teaching art in an elementary school starting in the fall. She was excited. However, there seemed to be something just below the surface that caused her some anxiety. Something that did not seem to fit with her plans. Pike noticed it as the week on the beach slipped away. He'd asked her a couple of times, but she said everything was great.

The week on Pelican Island was just what they needed. Time away from college, time with good friends, the beach, and great seafood, just before they headed back to college and their last set of final exams.

The last day on the beach, Tony and Pike sat in the rockers on the porch as Maggie and Julie went for one more swim before their departure in the early morning. The sun was high in the sky, and the shade of the porch was a welcome relief. Pike watched his friend shift around in his rocker. A couple times Tony got up and walked the length of the porch.

"Ok Tony, what's going on? Don't tell me nothing, I have known you too long to fall for that line." Pike sat back in his rocker and waited.

Tony stopped pacing and sat. He was quiet for a few minutes, then reached into his pocket and pulled out a small red box. Tony looked at his closest friend,

"I am going to ask her to marry me."

Pike stood up and hugged Tony.

"I'm so happy for you two. We have been wondering about what was going on between the two of you for the last few months."

If she says yes will you be my best man at our wedding?"

"What do you mean if she says yes, of course she will. Yes, I would be honored to be your best man." Tony and Pike sat and rocked for a while, each smiling. Pike thought about Maggie's ring, sitting in his desk at school. This was Tony and Julie's day, so he kept it to himself.

Pike watched the small waves march up the beach. So many thoughts raced around in his mind. He and Maggie had talked about the same things during the last few months.

Pike and Tony carried the last of the firewood from the cottage to an area in front of a sand dune. The fire caught hold and yellow orange flames lit up their faces. Tony and Pike sat around the fire on some driftwood logs, each lost in his thoughts.

Maggie and Julie came over the dune carrying everything needed to make smores. The ladies sat down on the only two lawn chairs that were in the cottage. The fire settled down into a rosy color, and the sparks seemed content to just flicker occasionally.

Tony pulled out a bottle of wine from the cooler sitting next to him. Pike passed around plastic glasses as Tony filled them. Pike raised his glass, "To our friendship, may it last forever, and may I pass Russian History."

Tony stood up, walked over to Julie, bent down in the sand, cleared his throat, and pulled the small red box out of his shorts.

"Julie, I have so enjoyed our journey for the last four years. I don't want it to end. I love you and would like this journey to continue. Will you marry me?"

Julie wiped a tear from her eye, reached out with both arms, hugged Tony, and whispered, "Yes." It was like everyone took a deep breath. Then Maggie jumped up, hugged Julie, then Tony. Pike embraced them both.

"I'm so happy for you guys," said Pike.

Maggie felt something inside of her that was disturbing, but it was just a feeling. Pike seemed happy for his friend.

4

BACK ON CAMPUS

The first days back on campus were difficult after spending spring break on Pelican Island. The two couples faced final exams, and the end of college in the next month.

Pike sat at his desk studying for his final in Russian History. He had a presentation to get ready for in his history class and he had a short story due in his creative writing class. He looked at his history textbook and the short story that sat at the edge of his desk.

Pushing away his work for the history class, he grabbed his short story. He put a fresh sheet of paper into his typewriter. Reading the last few lines of his story, the ending that he'd been searching for finally came to rest in his head.

Pulling the last page of his story out of the typewriter, he put the pages into his backpack. He got up from his desk, stretched and walked down the hall to Tony's room. A thin crack of light slipped under Tony's door. He knocked quietly.

"Go away, I'm studying." Tony's voice sounded tired. Pike knocked again, and heard the sound of Tony's chair scraping across the floor, followed by the sound of shoes stomping across the floor toward the door.

"This better be important!"

The door swung open, Tony shook his head at the sight of Pike.

"You look worse than I do.

"How about going to the student center for a shot of caffeine?" Pike stood looking at his friend, waiting for an answer.

"The student center does not close this week for a while."

Tony's voice seemed to wake up. The bell in the chapel struck ten. "We have about an hour," Tony said as he grabbed his Bolton College windbreaker. The door closed behind them as they made their way across campus to the student center.

"Have you finished studying for your Russian final?" Tony asked, knowing the answer already. Pike looked worried.

"You're going to study for that final tomorrow?" Tony sat, elbows on the table. Pike leaned back in his chair,

"I just cannot get excited about it, but I know I have to pass it to graduate." Pike's words were slow and deliberate. He and Tony finished their coffee and headed back to their dorm. Sleep did not come easily for Pike that night.

The next morning grades were posted in the hallway outside the Russian History classroom. Pike checked for his name and student number listed outside the Russian History classroom. Three or four students were milling around the list with the results of the final exam. Running his finger down the list, he smiled.

"Pike, you got the highest grade in the class again," grumbled one of the students in the class. One of the college football players kicked the waste basket sitting next to the wall. The dents in the wastebasket were a witness to other students' frustration with the results of their grades.

Pike walked out the door of Weaver Hall, the oldest building on campus with classrooms. The sun was starting to warm up the late spring day. Maggie was standing outside the student union with a group of her friends. She caught Pike's eyes, put up both arms, and tilted her head sideways. "Well?"

Pike walked over to her.

"Well, did you pass?" Maggie asked. Pike stood looking at her. He reached out and hugged her. "Highest grade in the class," said Pike as if it was no big deal. Reaching out, he took her hand and headed to the park across the street from the college. Through their years at Bolton they had spent a lot of time walking and talking in the park.

Strolling through the endless paths that crisscrossed throughout the park; he found their favorite bench. The trees were just beginning to green-up for summer.

Pike put his backpack on the bench, then sat down next to Maggie.

"Have you talked with my father?" She searched his face for an answer.

"No, I drove to your parents twice this week and parked across the street." Pike looked down at his sandals.

"You know you must ask him, he'll give you his blessing for our marriage. Maggie's eyes teared up. "Don't you want to marry me?"

"Maggie, of course I want to marry you. I love you; we have talked about it for the last three years." Pike squirmed on the bench. "But I don't have a job lined up after graduation like you and Tony. I have nothing to offer." Pike's voice got softer and softer until there was just silence.

Maggie reached out and took his hand. Her hands were warm and soft in Pike's hand. She looked up at him.

"You will get a job." Maggie's words were sure and strong. "Besides, my father likes you."

In Pike's dorm room, Maggie and Pike talked about their trip to Pelican Island and Tony and Julie long into the night. They both felt a little unsure of what to say. They both sensed a strong connection to each other and loved each other. The attraction never wavered since the first night they met at the autumn college dance their freshman year.

Maggie sat on the edge of Pike's bed and waited for Pike to say something. Pike sat in his desk chair facing her.

"I'm happy for Tony and Julie; I'm also a little scared." Pike sat back and watched Maggie.

"Me too, it's not that I don't love you, because I do deeply." Maggie's words came out slowly as she chose every word very carefully before letting it sneak out into the room.

Pike cleared his throat, and leaned in toward Maggie,

"I love you too; that has never changed. I don't have a job after we graduate in a few weeks." The words rushed without much control from Pike. The bond built from the day they met never changed. The words between them were selected very carefully. Over the years they had figured out how to talk about the difficult things.

Pike reached out and hugged Maggie as she put her hand on the door knob.

"I'll walk you back to your dorm, it's late." His words were like a warm blanket that felt so good on wintry nights. Maggie smiled and kissed him gently.

"Thank you, I feel like I need to just walk with my own thoughts."

Maggie walked back to her room in the quiet of the late night. The conversation with Pike was charged with emotion for both. As she walked she asked herself if she loved Pike, the answer surprised her, as it came from somewhere deep inside. A resounding yes. But it was other feelings that seemed to be growing inside.

After Maggie left to go back her dorm Pike sat down on his bed, and reached into the small drawer in his bureau. He had opened and closed the small box so many times since last summer he thought he might wear it out. Opening it one more time, he took out the small diamond ring. It still glimmered in the light.

He closed the box and sat with his back against the wall, turning the box over and over in his hands. He did not have a job, nor did he have any prospects for one after graduation. What could he give Maggie? He thought about Maggie having a job already and starting work in the early fall.

He envied Tony, who had a job waiting for him after graduation.

Opening the door to her room, she fell across her bed without even changing clothes. She was surprised when she felt tears coming. The bell in the chapel steeple struck midnight, but sleep still escaped her. She heard the bells from the chapel announcing 2:00 a.m. Finally, the faint rays of the sun began to creep in under the window shade. She looked out her window at the chapel standing tall and majestic with a few rays of the sun peeking around the steeple. On the steps of the chapel hidden from the sun, she saw someone sitting. When she looked again, the figure was gone.

Maggie blinked as the sun now poured through the window of her dorm room. Sitting up in bed she looked around her room, her roommate was still sleeping.

The phone rang in the hallway and a girl from across the hall answered it.

"Hey Maggie, your mother is on the phone, want me to tell her to call back?"

"No, I'll get it. Thanks." Grabbing the sweatshirt lying on her bed she walked to the phone.

"Hi Mom," Her voice still half asleep. "Yes, I can come home for a couple of days. Yes, I'll leave here about noon. Yes, I will fill up my car with gas. See you around noon."

The drive back home offered her a chance to clear her head. Graduation was only a few weeks away. It seemed like everything was moving too fast. Final exams, graduation, Tony and Julie getting married, Pike.

Maggie pulled up to her parents' house. She sat in her car for a few minutes, thinking about all the things going on in her life.

A pounding on the passenger window of her car, Betsy, her younger sister, laughed as Maggie jumped. Maggie slowly opened the door.

"You're home!" Betsy, Maggie's little sister, grabbed a suitcase from the back seat of the car.

As Maggie walked up the steps to the front door, her mother stepped outside,

"Are you catching a cold? Your voice sounded like you are. Maybe some hot tea would help."

Maggie didn't say anything, just hugged her mother.

The hall phone rang,

"Maggie, it's Pike." The voice of her younger sister broke through her thoughts.

"Tell him I will call him back." Her voice was tight, just above a whisper. Maggie stepped into the shower as the door to the bedroom she shared with her sister burst open, hitting the wall. "Pike said he would call you later. He won't be around a phone for the next few hours. He said he'd be in the library studying for the rest of his finals.

Maggie felt she had some space to think. She and Pike had been looking for a place to live after graduation. They had not talked to her father or mother. Pike was afraid her father would say no. He still did not have a job after graduation.

Maggie looked at a picture on her bureau, taken at their last formal dance. Someone had taken a picture of them standing facing each other. She and Pike stood lost in the others' eyes. It was as if the rest of the world had disappeared.

Slowly Maggie put the picture into the top dresser drawer under some sweaters. Then she closed the drawer.

5

THE BREAK UP

Maggie walked across the commons from her dorm to Carlson Student Center. She waved at a few friends making their way to breakfast, some fully awake others— all but sleep-walking. The birds were singing in the tall red Maple, just outside her dorm, a sure sign of the approach of summer.

The sun was just beginning to peek over the spire of the chapel. Maggie's mind was on the painting project in the spring art festival on campus.

Some of those making their way to breakfast looked rumpled, like they'd just rolled out of bed. Maggie dressed in white shorts and a light blue turtle neck sweater. She smiled as she thought about spring break a few weeks earlier and her time with Pike, Julie, and Tony.

Pushing her way through the doors to the student union, she greeted some students from her painting class. Groups of students, armed with coffee and doughnuts, settled in around tables with friends. They looked like they'd been up all-night working on their projects. Maggie knew she was behind in her own work.

Maggie looked around for Julie. She was not down for breakfast yet. Maggie found a small table next to the windows facing the chapel. A cup of black coffee and a blueberry muffin sat on the table with an array of books and notebooks spread out all over it.

Munching on a blueberry muffin, a petite blond-haired girl was making her way toward Maggie. As Maggie swallowed the first bite of the muffin she took a sip of her coffee. The girl stopped in front of Maggie's table. The girl wore a tight blue college t-shirt and jeans. "I'm Nancy. Are you Maggie?" she whispered. Without waiting to be invited to sit down she pulled a chair and sat staring at Maggie. "Like I said, my name is Nancy; Pike and I work together on Tapestry, the literary journal. We have become close. You've probably heard of me from Pike."

"No..." Maggie sat back wondering where this conversation was going. She stared across the table at the young woman sitting in front of her.

"Well, you know how love is, sometimes it just kinda smacks you in the face. Well, Pike and I love each other. He said he was over you. Well, I just wanted to tell you; he is mine now."

"Who are you again and what are you talking about?" Maggie held onto her anger; she was not going to let this person see her crack. Maggie leaned forward across the table; her brown eyes turned black as she drilled into Nancy's eyes. Nancy leaned back in her chair, her face red as she turned away from Maggie.

Maggie thought about throwing her drink in Nancy's face but did not want to waste good coffee. Nancy began to push her chair back. Maggie never broke eye contact with her.

Without another word she got up, turned, and joined two friends waiting at the stairs leading outside. Nancy and the other two girls started laughing as they pushed through the doors leading to the stairs.

⟫⟪◉⟫⟪

Nancy, the freshman cornering her in the cafeteria, had told Maggie she'd been with Pike last weekend. Pike had told her he was going home to visit his parents. When Maggie asked about his trip home, he was evasive, which was unlike him. There seemed to be a distance between them during the past week. He seemed to pull away when she reached out to hold his hand. He was hiding something. The conversation with Nancy seemed to fill in some spaces.

Pike sat at an oak table hidden away in a corner of the library, with books spread out in a semicircle around him. A light on the table created a small circle of light around his notes and an assortment of pens and pencils. Locking his hands behind his head, he leaned back in his chair, staring at the endless bookshelves filling the lower level of Watson Library.

He closed his eyes and thought about the young freshman girl who'd followed him around during the last few weeks. She reminded him of Maggie when she was a freshman—short blonde hair, deep brown eyes, and a smile that seemed to capture his attention. He thought about working together on Tapestry, the literary college journal. She clung to the male students working on the journal. Pike thought of talking about Nancy with the other people working. Pike thought about Nancy she was a scary girl whom he'd tried to stay away from.

He had told her he had a girlfriend, but it did not seem to deter her from her quest. Pike made the mistake of telling her she needed to stop following him. Pike had been sitting in the library when she walked up to his table. At first, Pike ignored her. She then sat down across from him and sat there staring at him. Finally, she stood up.

"Stop following me around campus, she yelled at Pike. "I am not interested in you."

People buried in the stacks stepped out to see what was going on. Pike looked at her with his mouth open. For once in his life he did not know what to say. He just sat glaring at the girl standing in front of him.

She turned, walked toward the stacks, and disappeared. Everyone seemed to go back to what they were doing except one person: Maggie's roommate, Carol. Slipping back into the stacks she wondered what that was all about. Carol could not wait to get back to her dorm room. She did not like Pike because he seemed to take all of Maggie's time.

Pike went back to work, trying to block the scene out of his head. Pike looked at the page he had been writing before the girl came to his table.

Graduation was only a week away and finals were almost over. He had not seen Maggie for a few days. She was at home with her parents for the weekend, and was going to be back on campus Sunday.

Pike packed up his notebooks and papers, threw them into his backpack, and left the library. Walking to the student union, he made his way to the bank of phones on the wall of the main floor of the union. For the second time, he could not contact Maggie.

Sunday morning, the phone rang on the wall just outside Pike's dorm room. Sleepily he stumbled out of bed, and opened the door to his room. He grabbed the phone, and with a voice heavy from sleep, he answered.

"Pike, is that you?" Maggie's voice sounded so far away,

"Maggie, where are you? I have been trying to contact you." There was a long hesitation.

"Pike, I trusted you," her voice was shaking. "I do not want to see you anymore. It is over." Her voice trembled as she spoke.

"What are you talking about? What is going on?" Pike's voice still groggy from sleep was fighting to understand what Maggie was saying.

"Maggie, I love you," Pike's voice was pleading. He knew Maggie was slipping away, but was not sure why.

Maggie said in a voice just above a whisper. "Don't try to contact me. I am going to stay with my family until graduation."

Pike sat in his room on the day of graduation. He had a letter from his parents saying they would not be able to make graduation. Pike's father had a big meeting that he had to attend. Pike's mother was concerned about his younger brother who was getting ready to head off to college.

Pike sat on his bed twisting his graduation cap around on his fingers. There were so many plans that he and Maggie had put together for this big day. A loud banging on his door pulled him away from his thoughts. It was Tony. "Pike, we need to be in the student union to line up for graduation."

Pike sat looking at his cap. He sat very still, He heard guys from the other rooms running down the stairs. Then the halls were quiet.

He sat on the floor with his knees pulled up to his chin. The sounds of people talking and laughing drifted in through his window.

Maggie arrived on campus with her family. Maggie wore a white skirt and a light blue blouse, carrying her graduation gown and cap. Her mother had her arm wrapped around Maggie's left arm. The family did not look happy.

Maggie's dad glanced up to Pike's dorm building. He knew that his daughter still loved Pike and whatever happened did not change that. He wanted to talk with Pike; he knew that Pike was hurting also. He had known Pike for four years and thought of him like a son.

The Commons of Bolton College was jammed with families and their children taking pictures. The empty chairs were beginning to fill up. Parents and graduates separated, and each went to their assigned seats. Tony searched for Pike. He debated one more time whether he should go up to Pike's room to see if he was there.

The band took their seats and graduates and their parents quieted as the President of Bolton College moved across the stage to the podium. Pike peeked out the window.

Wiping a stray tear from his cheek, he decided to join his friends in the ceremony. Grabbing his cap, he ran down the stairs and out the front door to his dorm. Racing toward the ceremony his black gown billowed out behind him as he ran. Making his way down the row of chairs he found his empty seat.

Julie was sitting in the row ahead of him. She did not make eye contact with Pike. During the ceremony he tried to make eye contact with Maggie, but she would not look toward him. The names were read after a short speech by the President of the college. As the graduates marched across the stage there was some clapping by excited parents. Maggie marched across the stage, her smile visible from where Pike sat waiting for his name to be called. Maggie's parents and some of her friends clapped as she shook hands with the President. She turned to return to her seat and looked at Pike. The smile was gone. Pike walked across the stage, no clapping. He took his paper from the President and kept on walking off the stage and back to his dorm.

6

ONE MORE TIME

Pike sat on his bed in his dorm room watching the breeze move the shades back and forth, gently knocking against the window jamb. The sounds of chairs being packed up in the commons slipped into his room. Graduation was over. College was over. Maggie was over.

"Pike, are you in there?" Tony's voice was accompanied by a loud pounding on his door. There was the sound of laughing and giggling as Tony and Julie pounded on the door. "Hey Pike, I know you are in there."

Pike sat quietly waiting for his best friend to get tired of pounding on the door and leave. "Pike, we are going to grab a burger in town, join us."

The sounds of footsteps faded away as Tony and Julie walked on the creaking floor of the old dorm. Pike got up from his bed and looked in the mirror,

"What is your next move, Pike?" Tony's words reverberated in Pike's brain. He knew Pike and Maggie went their separate ways immediately after graduation. But Tony knew that Pike didn't even know why.

Pike walked to the arboretum across the street from the college. Walking through the trees brought back many memories, too many to deal with. Sitting on one of the many benches along the wooded paths he sat watching a squirrel run across a limb of an old maple tree. It stopped just above the bench and looked down at Pike. The two stared at each other for a while. Neither moved. Pike watched as the squirrel ran up the tree and was lost in the red and orange leaves.

Pike got up and continued his walk along the paths. The sounds of the trees whispering with the gentle summer breeze, the smells of summer permeated his senses. Maggie's face jumped into his mind, memories began to flood back. The question of what happened played itself out over and over as he walked back to his dorm.

The sound of someone pounding on his door woke him from a restless sleep. Bruce Mason's voice invaded his room.

"Hey Pike, you got a package." Pike opened the door. Resting on the floor were two packages---one a large package wrapped in brown wrapping paper, the other a thick envelope marked special delivery.

A letter from his parents:

> Pike,
> Sorry we could not make your graduation. You know how busy we are getting your brother ready for college and working on our business. We knew you would understand. When are you coming home? We got your room all fixed up for you when you return. Your father has been using it as his office. Your father talked with your former boss at the Stone House Restaurant and he is willing to let you work there during the summer.
> We hope to meet Maggie, the girl that you have been talking about for the last three years. Well, you know how people drift apart after they graduate from college. Most college relationships end with graduation.
> Well we sent you some money to get you home.
> Your father

A letter from the college informed him he would have to move out of his room within one week after graduation.

"Hey Pike, are you in there?" Pike opened the door and Tony walked in and sat on the bed.

"Pike, I'm sorry about you and Maggie. Have you heard from her?"

Pike shook his head. "Tony, when are you leaving for Pelican Island?"

"That's what I wanted to talk to you about; my parents are traveling this summer and will not be in the cottage all summer. I was wondering what your plans are and if you are interested in spending the summer on the island?"

For the first time since graduation, Pike smiled at the thought of going to Pelican Island again. Tony and Pike had spent many good times there.

"Yes."

Tony and Pike sat in Pike's room talking about the adventures they' had enjoyed there during their years at college. Tony knew that Pike was hurting from the break up with Maggie.

Tony ran to his room next door to Pike's room, and came back with a bottle of wine. Tony pulled the cork and poured two Dixie cups half full, held his cup up in the air.

"To graduation, to past good times, and future good times.

Pike held up his cup "to new adventures" as Tony's words filled the room. For the first time Pike thought about something besides Maggie. They each emptied their cups and refilled them.

Tony packed up his belongings the next morning and shipped his college things to Pelican Island. He grabbed a 12:30 flight to the island.

Pike tried once more to contact Maggie before he left for the island. He walked up the steps to her front door, reached out to knock on the door when it opened. It was Maggie's little sister.

"He's here again." She turned around and walked away from the door, leaving Pike standing on the front steps. After what seemed like a lifetime, Maggie came to the door. She stepped outside.

"Why are you here?" her voice was cold. She looked like she had not slept well.

"I am leaving and just wanted to say goodbye." His words caught in his mouth. She looked at him. So many memories rushed into her head. They stood looking at each other; the words would not come.

"I don't know what happened to us. I love you; I trusted you with my heart." Maggie's words caught Pike by surprise.

He said, "But at least listen…" but Maggie had turned and walked back into the house. She closed the door, and leaned against it. Tears forced their way out and ran down her cheeks. Maggie's mother put her arms around her daughter and hugged her as they walked into the living room. Maggie let it all go as she leaned into her mother's shoulder.

Pike walked down the sidewalk, turned, and looked back at the house. In the window in the front of the house, Maggie's little sister stuck her tongue out. He turned, walked away. He knew Maggie had closed her door to him. He kept thinking about her last words to him "trusted with all her heart." That hurt the most, he'd never betrayed her.

Pike's car was full of everything he owned. Rolling down the window of his car he drove away toward Pelican Island.

Maggie spent a few days after graduation at home with her family. She had seen Pike a few times on campus but had avoided him.

"I am pregnant!" The words exploded from her lips as she looked into her mirror. She stared at her reflection. They'd been so careful. Maggie sat on the edge of her bed, put her hands over her face, tears leaking through her fingers. She had been concerned when she did not get her period. It had always arrived like clockwork. She became anxious and Pike noticed that there was something different about her the last few weeks. In the heat of a moment, they had not used protection as they made love in Pike's dorm room, during a day of senior finals.

Pike had awakened early in the morning with Maggie snuggled up against him. Pike just lay there listening to Maggie softly breathing. Pike leaned over and kissed her on her forehead.

"Maggie turned over, opened one eye. Pike was motionless, watching her.

"Good morning, Pike. I like waking up next to you." Her words were no more than a whisper in Pike's ear.

<hr />

One Sunday afternoon a few months later, Maggie sat with her parents and told them she was pregnant. As she expected, her father became terribly upset and asked where Pike was?

"I broke it off with him. He does not know about it." She lowered her eyes as she told her father the story of the break up. Maggie sat on the couch in the living room with her parents. There was no sound, just the squeak of her father's shoes as he paced back and forth in the living room. Maggie's mother reached out and pulled Maggie's father to sit down on a chair across the room from the couch.

"Are you telling me he knows nothing about his future baby?" Maggie's father said as once again he started pacing the floor. Maggie's mother looked at her daughter. Do you have a plan?"

"I have a teaching job in Lakewood and will move there starting in the fall. I'm sorry; I know this is not the plan that you had for me. I'm so sorry."

"Do you still love Pike?" Maggie's mother's words were spoken gently.

I don't know what I feel right now."

Maggie's father and mother got up from their chairs and sat on either side of Maggie. Her mother put her arm around her daughter, and tears flowed freely from Maggie and her parents.

"I hate Pike!" shouted Maggie's younger sister who had been listening to every word spoken. She came in and sat next to her mother.

7

OPENING NEW DOORS

Pike leaned back in his chair, and looked across the class-room. It had been twenty years since graduation, and since he had talked with Maggie. After a painful six months, he stored all the pictures and letters from his college years with Maggie in his parents' house. Tony and Julie called him and invited him down during the first summer after graduation, he decided it was too soon. He had not called them or heard from them in the last two years.

Pike was surprised when he received another phone call from Tony inviting him down for a men's two weeks. Julie was going to be visiting her family back in Illinois. Pike sent a letter to Tony thanking him for the invitation. A phone call from Tony a few days later offered a good excuse for going.

"Hey Pike, good to hear from you. Got a project we can work on. Front porch needs fixing, are you up for it?" said Tony.

"Tony sounds like fun, I'll bring my tools. It will be good to get together again always enjoy working on projects." By the end of the phone call Pike was as excited as Tony.

———◦((◦))◦———

The school year as a teacher was over; the students had left for the summer. He erased the blackboard, as Duke, the maintenance man, walked in to empty the wastebasket.

"Well, mister Pike, what are you going to do for the summer?" Duke's words came slowly, each word seemingly ruminated before putting it together into a complete sentence.

"Going down to Pelican Island for a couple of weeks to help my college buddy rebuild the front porch on his cottage."

"Next year is your last year, I hear."

"Yeah, one more year; I am retiring, it has been more than twenty-five years. Time to do something new."

"Well, I'll miss you -you're one of the few teachers who speaks to me."

Duke turned, shuffled out of the room.

Pike closed his gradebook, turned in his grades, filled a few boxes with personal objects from his desk. Holding a box under one arm and his backpack slung over his shoulder, he looked at the empty desks. It had been a good year.

A few teachers were getting together after school at Cathy's Tavern for some free appetizers and a couple of beers.

Pike put the box behind the seat in his truck, headed for the tavern, then stopped.

Pike was torn between stopping and spending some time with his friends or getting on the road. The pull of the sand and sea was stronger than the pull to stop and talk with his friends.

There was a strong cool breeze from the north; he shivered a little as he got into his truck. Shaking his shoulders, he shrugged off a feeling that he was missing something. Putting it out of his thoughts, he started his truck and took off for Pelican Island.

Section Two

8

PELICAN ISLAND

The first thing one notices driving across Salt Marsh Bridge from the mainland to Pelican Island is the pungent smell of mud and salt marshes lining each side of the bridge. Foamy tides of the Atlantic reach up into the island, creating backwaters filled with birds and kayakers. The hectic rush of the mainland drains away as you drive over the bridge onto the island.

Spanish moss hangs from the old oaks lining the main thoroughfares through the island, catching the sea breezes. They sway back and forth in a rhythm that matches the rhythm of the people living on the island.

The Atlantic's personality changes with the seasons. In the summer, the heat is intense, and a strong sea breeze is a welcome relief for tourists flocking to the beaches.

The white sand of the beaches stretches as far as the human eye can see. Natural sand dunes create a boundary between the ocean and the beach homes. Some houses appear modest. Others seem to be pushing the bounds of extravagance in appearance and opulence.

The houses built in the early forties, fit into a much gentler life and scale of living. Summer cottages passed from one generation to the next; treasured for their simplicity and an escape from the more hectic world on the mainland.

During college, Pike, Maggie, Julie, and Tony had made their way to Pelican Island during spring breaks and a couple of times during the summer when classes were light. They always stayed at Tony's parents' small cottage in an older section of the Island. Much had remained unchanged over the years. Cottages built in the 1920s had been renovated; however, the exterior features stayed the same.

Tony's parents' grandparents built their cabin in the late 1920s. It was simple: a living room, one bedroom, a small kitchen, and a bathroom. The favorite part of the cabin was the front porch built by Tony's grandparents. Grandpa Ed was a handyman as were many of the men living in the row of cottages. They helped each other with building, electrical, and plumbing issues over the years.

Most of the cottages had a name on a sign above the porch. So, it was with Tony's grandparents.

Tony's grandfather carved the name Windscape onto a piece of driftwood, he found on one of his sunrise strolls along the beach.

Tony's father added an attic bedroom to the cottage for Tony and friends who always seemed to end up staying overnight. It had a large window facing the sea and the room was high enough to see over the sand dunes to a wide-open view of the sea.

With each new generation, there were changes and updates. The bedroom put up in the attic, a new bathroom, updated electrical wiring, and plumbing.

People walking the beach every morning accompanied by their dogs continued a ritual started by great-grandparents.

Today's walkers, or the "regulars" as the newcomers on the island call them, were now reaching into the low rungs of their early sixties. They were yesterday's children who once played on the beaches. Today, there were fewer children in the cottages, adult grand-children had neither the time nor inclination to visit the small cottages belonging to their parents and grandparents.

They did not seem to be interested in the island's slow pace. Today instead of small kids running and playing in the surf, there were the regulars and their dogs, dogs running and playing in the surf with much barking and much tail wagging.

The beach sat in front of small white, one and two-bedroom cottages. Summer homes stood the test of time against the onslaught of the Atlantic storms and bulldozers of the development companies.

Every morning, a group of friends formed over a lifetime walked the beach, looking for treasures left by the morning tide. The conversations were rich with subtleties born of years of walking and talking together; shared family events bridging both the good and sad times that had invaded their lives. A lifetime of sharing had welded the regulars into a close-knit group who shared the early morning sand with their assortment of dogs. All shapes and sizes—dogs jumping, barking and even waging war with the endless marching waves tearing at the beach. All different breeds, and not a designer dog in the group.

9

INTRODUCTION TO JOHN AND THE REGULARS

The fingers of the sun were just reaching over the horizon of the Atlantic. John stepped off his porch, as the regulars headed toward his cottage. Some sipped coffee or tea from their mugs. Others carried water bottles. Swirling around them were the assortment of dogs ranging from a belly dragger named Sam to a big coal-black dog named Goliath, the most laid-back gentle dog in the group. Mr. Bud, a liver colored Brittany spaniel with gray whiskers like his owner, John, sat on the porch watching the other dogs.

John gave Bud a couple of scratches behind his ears, and then commanded him to go. Mr. Bud took off, joining his friends as they roamed the beach, running, chasing, playing.

John waited for the group to reach his house. "Good morning," he said, with his usual high energy, which seemed to appear as soon as he opened his eyes in the morning. He looked around at the group. It was obvious some were not morning people. Rachel was an exception. Like John, she awoke in the morning with energy bubbling over.

She smiled at John, raised her mug, and said "hello" with a voice that seemed unusually warm. He smiled back. The group walked down the beach, talking, and laughing, each one enjoying the others' company.

Early morning, their favorite part of the day: the beach was a clean slate, awaiting the sounds of kids' laughter and sandcastles, footprints, and memories of a day's escapades. The beach was empty, except for a few people walking alone and a few solitary runners with earphones, oblivious to the scenery around them.

Clusters of sea gulls played tag with the pounding surf of the incoming tide. The dogs took off full throttle chasing the gulls, creating a lot of barking and squawking as the birds took flight.

John, the oldest member of the group, was also the local historian. Often, he conversed with tourists, answering their questions about the island's history and the cottages in this one small area. He had a habit of stroking his beard before delving into a story. Sometimes he got in the middle of a story and a tourist would interrupt and ask about a good place for dinner.

The regulars walked, shared stories of their lives, and laughed their way through their morning walk. Beatrice Reynolds in the middle of her conversation, with Franny Belmont, bumped into Rachel Hancock, who had stopped walking a few steps in front of her.

"Excuse me, Rachel, maybe you should put some brake lights on your hips." The group laughed. Rachel fumed inside.

Rachel turned to John.

"So, John who's renting your cabin for the summer?" All eyes turned to him. John always felt that Rachel should have been an investigative news reporter.

"A woman from Chicago, who used to come down here in the summer and spring break when she was in college. She is a friend of Tony and Julie."

"What does she do? How long is she staying?" Questions poured out of her mouth faster than John could answer. There were smiles around the group; some felt sorry for John, having been themselves on the receiving end of her questions.

Rachel looked up to see John had kept walking. "John, wait," but he kept walking. It was no use. Rachel jogged up beside him, continuing with questions about the renter.

"Rachel, I don't know any more about her, except a friend of

Tonys knows her and vouches for her." All Tony said was she is a teacher turned artist." As quickly as Rachel had asked her questions, Rachel turned her attention back to the group. Hoping he escaped a further barrage, John turned his attention to the dogs as they chased each other and the gulls.

As the morning began to warm, regulars turned and started moving back in the direction of their homes. One by one they peeled off and disappeared into their houses. The dogs, one by one, followed their masters.

John was the last to leave. He looked up to see his white cottage in the distance. As he walked, he was thankful for the quiet of the morning without Rachel's constant questioning.

Next to his house was the small cottage he had bought a few years ago, fixed up, and turned into a rental. Over the years, he had upgraded it. The only thing left to do this summer was repaint the house before his renter for the summer arrived.

Mr. Bud walked along beside him as he walked past his house and up two steps to the front porch of his rental. The sunbaked tips of a faded white fence peeked above the drifting sands. The front porch and sand dunes stood guard between the house and the ever-present sea.

John and Bud walked up on the porch. Bits of sand left an almost invisible track from the steps to a white rocker. He pulled one of the two white rockers forward, sat down and watched the pelicans swooping and disappearing beneath the surface of the water. They resurfaced with a fish dangling from their beaks.

Tired from his morning romp, Bud lay down with a loud thump near John's rocker. Reaching down, John put his hand on the dog's head. Bud looked up. John and Bud had been together long enough to read each other's body language. John went into the cottage and came back with a pan of water. As John continued to rock, he thought about the painting he should be doing. Then thought, well, maybe tomorrow.

As the sun began to invade the porch, John and Mr. Bud went next door to John's house for breakfast. John put down another pan of water for Bud, walked out the back door and into a small shed that was his workshop.

He switched on the lights and air-conditioning. The shed had a familiar aroma of fresh shavings and wood; it took John back to when he was a kid and he would come out to this shop with his father. There were strong memories as he stood looking at the assortment of tools filling his shop. A small cradle stood on the workbench against a wall. Tools spread out along the bench, a witness to the progress of his work. John smiled as he thought of his father, would never leave his tools out at the end of a day. Looking at his bench, then off into the distance, with a smile he said,

"Sorry, Dad." He could see his father smiling back.

The air conditioner sucked the heat out of the workshop. John sat looking at a small cradle sitting on the workbench he was making for a neighbor and her granddaughter. Running his hand over the top of the cradle, he smiled. It was smooth as glass, with the three coats of varnish applied in the last few days. The sounds of a hand saw filled the space in the small workshop as John worked on a spindle that would make up the back of the cradle.

10

THE STRANGER

Early one morning, the regulars on their morning trek noticed a man walking alone in the distance. He seemed preoccupied with his thoughts as he carried a backpack over one shoulder and what seemed to be a tall drink from the nearby shop. The stranger walked just inside a space between the sand dunes and the wide-open beach. The regulars watched him, and conversation spread through the group, each asking if they knew who the stranger was or if anyone had seen him before. The dogs, oblivious to the change in tempo and pace of their masters, kept chasing and retreating from the incoming waves

John said he thought he had seen the man sitting in the same place at sunset on an old driftwood tree trunk. He seemed to be staring at something in the distance.

John made a half turn and looked at the regulars. Rachel stood looking at the man sitting on the tree trunk.

"Well, I am going to find out who he is and why he is here," said Rachel. She waited about a half minute. No one else volunteered. She took three steps, and John stepped in front of her, with some degree of irritation in his voice,

"He's not bothering anyone; why don't we just leave him alone." With the words just leaving John's mouth, Mr. Bud took off at a dead run toward the man sitting on the tree trunk. John glared at

Rachel and started walking fast toward the man and calling Bud, who seemed to be on a mission.

The group watched Bud running. The dog stopped about three feet from the stranger, butt up in the air, his head resting on his front paws. Bud's eyes never left the newcomer.

Without looking at the dog, the stranger started talking to him.

"Hello dog, how are you this morning?" Bud sat down and stared at the man. John stopped about twenty steps away. The newcomer put his hand down near the sand. Bud, always curious, slowly walked up and sniffed his hand. Satisfied, Bud turned his attention to John, now a few feet away.

"Sorry about my dog. He's just the friendly sort," John said. The man gently pulled his hand up and continued reading his book.

"Not afraid of dogs," the man said, without looking at John. The man reached down, took a sip of his drink, sat it back on the tree trunk, and went back to reading his book as if John was not there. "Sorry about the interruption," John muttered as he turned and headed back toward the regulars. The man made no movement indicating any awareness of John's presence. John turned, called to his dog.

The regulars walked further down the beach with their eyes on the stranger, as John walked slowly back to the group. Rachel squirmed, almost unable to wait for John to catch up the group.

"Well?" her words shot out toward John, who was still at least ten feet away. John said nothing as he closed the gap between himself and the group. Rachel stood, her arms across her chest, waiting.

The stranger put his book down and sipped the last gulps of his drink, watching the waves roll in toward the beach. He glanced over at the group walking with their dogs. Reaching into his backpack he pulled out a letter from Tony and Julie, in Italy. Carefully, he opened it and read it for the fourth time in the last two days.

He reread the last line of the letter again even though he had memorized it.

"I hope you will enjoy your summer on the island. I am sure it will raise a lot of memories for you. Remember the old memories and be open to creating new ones. Remember there are always two sides to every story."

The stranger put the letter back into its envelope, folded it in half, and put it back into his backpack. Once more he watched the group of people and their dogs retracing their way to the cottages. Taking out his journal, he wrote down what he was seeing on the beach and his thoughts.

With the first tourists arriving, the stranger picked up his empty cup and backpack and made his way over the dunes to Tony's home.

When John and Bud rejoined the group, they circled around him and all started asking questions. Rachel's voice rose above the rest, which always amazed him. Rachel was only about five feet tall, yet the voice coming out of her mouth always made him think she had been a strong teacher with good control over her middle-school students.

Rachel's badgering prevented John from sharing his thoughts that the stranger might be a friend of Tony and Julie. Rachel finally stopped firing questions. Approaching her house, the group stopped as she walked up the steps to her porch. She turned before she went inside her house to give John one more Rachel look.

John smiled as the group continued their walk back to their houses. The dogs, reluctant to part with their buddies, had to be coaxed to rejoin their masters and end their morning romp. John's house was farthest down the beach and a little isolated from the others.

Walking alone toward his house with the dog, he thought about the first time he was introduced to the regulars. He was considered a newcomer because his family had owned their cottage for only one generation. It had been purchased by his parents and given to him when they passed away a few years earlier.

After the loss of his wife and retiring from his job, John reopened the old cottage. Then came a few years of commuting back and forth from Savanna. Finally, he decided to cut his ties with the past and the city at the same time. He moved into his family's cottage, put in some sweat equity, updated the electrical system, and added a new fireplace.

The first time he met the regulars, there were a lot of questions from the group about his family. Where did he come from? Who were his parents? Most questions came from the sandy-haired little spitfire of a woman named Rachel. She had a sparkle in her eyes when she spoke and a smile that changed her countenance in the space of a heartbeat.

Sometimes, annoyed by her bombardment of questions that seemed to rain down upon him, John wondered if she ever took a breath, and would turn his attention to others in the group. Rachel just continued and did not seem to care if anyone was listening. She talked so fast, John figured there must be an ON button from some portion of her brain to her mouth, and decided right there he would stay away from her and concentrate on the other regulars.

As John walked up the two steps from the sand to his front porch, he caught himself thinking about the stranger. There was a time, when he first arrived on the island; he was the stranger and the one that seemed to be on the outside. John made plans to learn more about the new guy and help him fit into life on the island.

Buddy shot past him as he opened the screen door and the dog headed straight for his water bowl by the kitchen stove. Looking at his best friend, John decided a cold glass of water or maybe some iced tea might be just the right thing for him to finish off his morning walk.

The sun was high enough in the sky to begin heating the interior of his house. It was time to open some windows and let the sea breezes fill the room with cooler air and the sweet smell of the vast body of water a few hundred yards beyond his porch. The low sand dunes covered with sea grasses waved in the midmorning breeze off the endless sea. Depending on the wind and storms, the dunes changed from year to year. However, they always stood as protection against the temperamental sea.

After a moment of reflection on the morning, John sat down at his computer and connected with his email friends from everywhere he had ever traveled. John used his computer to find the best travel deals. Unlike some of his neighbors, he liked to escape and see other parts of the world.

11

RENTER

In early February, John had placed a flyer for a summer rental of the cottage next to him. There had been a few responses over the winter months, but the inquiries had trickled to one or two a month. In conversations with those answering the ads, none seemed to fit the person John was looking for. In early March, he received an interesting response to the flyer.

The cottage had been vacant for many years. The owners were children of one of the regulars who had passed away a few years ago. The adult children had visited the cottage only once in the last few years. They were eager to sell and put the money into something else that would fit their lifestyle.

John had bought the house for two reasons. One to control who moved in next to him and the other to rent the house during the summer months. Renting out the small cottage was to be his travel money.

Pulling up the response to his flyer, John read the note from his friend about the prospective tenant. She was about the same age as John and an artist who needed to get away from Chicago for a while. John's friend said he had met her, had lunch with her, and was sure she would be a good tenant. A telephone number and an email address gave John the option of contacting her. "Hello, my name is John Polk, I understand you're interested in renting a cottage on Pelican Island."

12

As the morning light grew brighter, Maggie opened her eyes and looked at the electric clock on the faded white willow end table beside her bed. Stretching her long arms over her head, she pulled back the sky-blue covers, placed her feet on the floor. Running her fingers through her brown hair with a few strands of gray peeking out, she headed for the bathroom. With a quick glance, she moved in closer to the mirror, looking at the fine lines around the corners of her eyes. For a moment she wondered who the person was looking back at her.

The years had been kind to her but the thieves of age had created a few wrinkles. However, the fire in her eyes was still visible, even in the small light above the bathroom mirror.

Grabbing a faded Bolton College sweatshirt and a pair of well-worn shorts, she headed to the kitchen following the smell of fresh brewed coffee, picked up her favorite mug from the open cabinet above the kitchen sink, and she poured her coffee. Holding her cup with one hand, she slowly ran the mug across her forehead.

Stepping onto the screened porch facing the beach, she sipped her coffee. The smell of strong morning coffee and the pungent salty ocean air surrounded her as she stepped down onto the cool sand slipping between her toes. She made her way toward the beach.

The gentle slap of the morning tide filled in the space around her. A new feeling seemed to be gathering strength inside her from the first day she had arrived at the beach house. Deep in her gut, it seemed to be more of a need than a feeling. A need to paint once again. This was something that seemed to have dried up in the rush of teaching in Chicago.

An all too familiar pull from somewhere deep inside to get back to a painting, started a few days ago. Turning around, she walked slowly back to the cottage, the sounds of the ocean receding into the background. Stopping on the first step, she shook the sand from her feet. In the corner of the porch, her easel beckoned her back to work. Just as quickly, the tug pulling her back to the cottage and her painting was gone. Turning her back on her easel, Maggie refilled her cup and stood looking at the sandy beach and ocean stretching out beyond.

Maggie opened the door to the porch and headed toward the beach. The sand, having accepted some of the sun's warmth, slipped between her toes. Being mid-morning, it would not be possible to walk on the beach without her sandals. Raising her cup to her lips she sipped the remaining coffee. Putting her hand to her forehead to protect her eyes from the growing strength of the sun, she looked down the beach. His back to her, a lone figure played tag with the incoming tide as he walked. His head was bent down as if studying something in the sand at his feet. Bending down he picked something up and studied it for a moment then gently placed it back in the sand. Suddenly her stomach tightened, gripping her in a tight spasm. Something about his gait, something familiar yet at the same time foreign.

Turning, she walked in the opposite direction. Waves washing over her feet brought her back to the present and the pull of her easel resting alone on the porch. The presence of the stranger walking the beach lodged in her memory the rest of the morning. Searching her memory did not solve the mystery; it only left her with an uneasiness. She stared at the house she had rented for the summer, she thought about all the promises that she'd made to herself about returning to her painting; Maggie reluctantly headed back to the porch. The all too familiar push pull feelings began to surface again. The pull of her artistic side and the push away, sometimes equally as strong. Armed with a glass of iced tea, standing in front of her painting from a few days ago, some colors jumped out at her. A new wave of excitement rushed through her. With a quick push of her hair behind her ears she sat on a stool in front of her painting. The brushes once lying dormant at the side of her painting began to fly across the canvas. Colors from her pallet, each added warmth and life to the painting.

Time slowed its pace. Lost in her work, her inner voice stopped for a little while. Minutes turned to hours. As hours slipped away, the canvas began to evolve into a series of images.

That night, sleep finally came. Maggie's need to create, now satisfied for the moment, allowed her to fall into a deep sleep. Faces and images swirled around her subconscious demanding her attention.

Faces and emotions long buried raced to be seen and felt with all the intensity of the first day of spring.

13

ike was up at five and on the beach long before most other people had stirred in their beds. The morning was overcast, the wind slipped in during the night, whipping the waves into a fury as they slammed into the complacent sand on the beach. Finding a driftwood trunk of a tree propped up against a low rise of sand dunes, he settled in for the morning. His floppy hat pulled down, covering the top half of his face. This morning pulled a little tighter against small sand particles riding on the wind's breath.

The call from Tony, his college roommate. They had shared marriages and divorces with each other, and it seemed to create a connection not broken neither by either time or circumstance. When Tony called and asked Pike to do him a favor and watch his house in Pelican Island, it was easy to say yes. Tony and his wife, Julie, would be taking off for a world tour to celebrate their twenty-fifth wedding anniversary. The request from Tony could not have come at a better time for Pike. He finished his career as a middle school teacher and decided to put all his efforts into writing full time. At first, there was a thrill in being able to devote all his time to writing, a lifelong goal. Lately the writing had stopped, and the blank sheets of paper outnumbered the sheets filled with words.

During time spent at his oak desk, his attention seemed focused on other things. The shrubs in his back yard needed his attention. Or walking through his home and into his workshop, something beckoned him to spend time there. Everything seemed to be working together to get him away from his desk. Writing now became a chore instead of a thrill.

Pike said a silent thank you to whomever was listening for the opportunity to escape Chicago and all the distractions that seemed to exist. Looking around his office and the pile of papers and blank sheets of paper, he made the decision quickly. He would pack up his old truck and head to Pelican Island in the next couple of weeks. He had decided to escape. The decision made cleared the cobwebs from his mind, allowing him to sense new possibilities.

The days passed quickly and soon Pike took his first step out of Tony's cottage and onto the beach. Even though it was still the end of June, the air held a promise of warmth and the mixed aromas of sand and sea welcomed him. Looking at the waves creeping toward the beach, row after row, as far as he could see; he knew he had made the right decision to leave Chicago for a while.

Walking the beach in the morning, clutching his coffee and his backpack slung over his shoulder, little did he know eyes were watching and wondering. The beach stretched out before him with only the natural sounds of nature.

The coffee, still steaming in his mug, spread a warm feeling throughout Pike's body. There was a stirring of something inside which he had not felt for a while: a desire to write.

As he walked, an expansive driftwood log leaning against a sand dune invited Pike to come and rest for a while. As he sat there, he watched a flock of sea gulls hunt for food amongst the debris washed up during the changing tides. He marveled at their ability to watch the incoming waves, keep an eye on the wet sand at their feet and still find things to eat. The flock looked like they were performing a dance in which they all knew the steps.

Pike reached the steps to his cottage, walked up and past the screen door to the porch. He tossed the backpack onto an empty chair. Glancing at his desk in the living room, he realized the words that had flowed so freely on the beach had dried up and blown away like the sand on his porch.

The sun crept out from behind a cloud with a promise of warm weather. The sounds of screaming children and the laughter of families drowned out the sound of waves and the screeches of the gulls and black pelicans.

The regulars were not sure where Pike had come from. Some said it had something to do with another life he had lived before he showed up on Pelican Island. Pike was one of those people whose age was difficult to ascertain. He could have been anywhere from forty to mid-sixties. The lines on his face chronicled the events of his life. Each one with a story to tell if Pike had been willing to share his past. They said Pike just showed up one day. It was like he knew the place but just had not been around for a while. He was always alone, seemed satisfied with his own company, and did not need others. Walking alone on the beach in the mornings, one would usually see him sitting on a driftwood tree trunk dressed in a faded green college T-shirt, cut off blue jeans and sandals. A grey beard, partially covering the bottom part of his face, hid it from the rays of the sun. Pike's faded hat covered his head, and his ears, and the back of his neck. Usually Pike sat watching the rolling ocean. Some say he was looking for something. It was all speculation because Pike never spoke to the early morning wanderers strolling along the deserted morning beach. It seemed his one indulgence was a morning latte from the local coffee shop, which he held in both hands in front of him as he sipped slowly. Some said he was a writer or a photographer. He always had a camera or a pad of paper with him. Those who passed him every morning said that either he was drawing or writing in his journal. When the early morning regulars gathered, Pike's name would come up and there was much speculation about him. Who was he and where did he come from?

John and his dog, Bud, part of the early morning group, chose to approach Pike and find out some answers to all their speculation.

As was his usual morning routine, Faces and emotions long buried raced to be seen and felt with all the intensity of the first day of spring. The morning was overcast with clouds hanging low in the sky. The wind had ridden in on the morning tides, whipping the waves into a frenzy as they slammed the beach and receded. Finding his personal driftwood tree trunk braced against the low rise of sand dunes and armed with his coffee mug, he settled in for the morning. His floppy hat was pulled down tightly against the battering of the wind. Bits and pieces of sand rode on the waves of the surging Atlantic breezes.

He loved feeling his smallness against the vast ocean, stretched out in front of him. His eyes were glued to the endless marching white caps as they pounded the white sands of the beach. He leaned back and relaxed, oblivious to the gathering regulars walking the beach as the sun finally appeared in the morning sky.

"His name is Mr. Bud and he's my ambassador to everyone on the beach." Simultaneously, John reached out to shake hands. Pike ignored John, returning his attention to the ocean and movement of the waves. Waiting for what seemed like a lifetime, John pulled his hand back. Mumbling something incomprehensible, John turned, leaving a reluctant Mr. Bud behind. For a moment Pike watched the shrinking image of John and Mr. Bud continuing their morning walk. With a tinge of regret, Pike refocused on the ever-changing attack and retreat—the assault of the sea against the land. Returning his gaze and concentration back to the two figures, Pike wondered which he regretted more the shrinking image of the man or the dog. Pike thought back to another day and time when she would be sitting with him. The fading image of her brown hair and matching brown eyes filled his mind. For a moment, and only a moment, a smile formed in the corner of his mouth. Just as quickly it faded away, replaced by an expressionless stare at the scene before him. The screech of two sea gulls fighting over a small crab washed upon the shore brought him back to the present. Slowly gathering up his backpack and the cold dregs of his morning coffee, Pike stood and moved down the beach. The subtle tentacles of age had slowly made themselves known. Families were gathering on the beach, with the high-pitched screams of their small children playing tag with the waves. It was time to move on.

As the regulars grouped for their morning walk each day,

questions occasionally focused again on him and his identity? He was now the resident mystery. Where did he come from? Most of the questions came from Rachel. In fact, she persisted in her quest for answers. This morning she placed herself strategically next to John as they began their trek down the beach. John could not help but notice her matching his strides, which was difficult for her short legs.

John tried to focus his attention on Mr. Bud, who sensed something and stayed next to John instead of frolicking with his friends, chasing the waves and exploring crabs washed upon the sand.

"John, I know you can hear me." Rachel's voice was difficult to ignore, especially when she was walking just to his left. Reluctantly, John turned to face her as she struggled to keep up with him. She turned, squared her shoulders against the wind, and looked directly into John's eyes. The other regulars watched and felt a drop of pity for him, as Rachel put her hands on her hips and shouted,

"John, we think you should find out who this guy is. Whatever you can learn about him. I know you've tried but everybody still thinks you would have the best chance of getting the facts."

The rest of the group members turned and tried to look anywhere except at John. Some of the regulars even shook their heads, hoping he would see they were not part of this ambush. Even though they would not have asked John, other regulars were curious also. A few of them were relieved Rachel had not focused on them.

John turned to face the others in the group with whom he'd been meeting every morning rain or shine for the last three years. His voice was soft but tinged with authority. "His name is Pike. I don't know if that is his first or his last name. Tony told me some stories about when he and Pike were in college together.

Based on the stories, they had great adventures. John was with Tony before he and Julie left for their anniversary cruise. He told me Pike, a friend from college, would be watching their house for the summer. He did not share any more information about him."

Stepping back, Rachel could not help but smile. She had learned

---

some information about the stranger walking on her beach. John knew that the information would only be a momentary reprieve. Rachel would want to know more. Satisfied, she turned her attention back to the group.

Feeling neglected, the dogs began barking with a different level of intensity, causing the conversation to stop abruptly. As they turned toward the barking dogs, they saw them running in circles around something on the wet sand. John and a couple of the other men in the group stared. A few called their dogs, but the dogs paid no heed. All the dogs' attention focused on the sand in front of them. When the men finally were close enough, they saw what was causing the commotion. In the middle of the pack was a large horseshoe crab, obviously battered by incoming waves.

John walked between the dogs as the other men pulled their animals away from the crab. He bent over and, using a stick, John turned the crab over. It was still alive but not in decent shape. The best chance for it was to get back into the ocean, but the waves would not allow that to happen. John reached down, gently picked up the crab, and waded into the surf. When he was about knee deep, he placed it into the water and made his way back the beach. The crab, beat up by the tide, probably would not live long. However, it certainly would have become lunch for the gulls that circled overhead.

As the men made their way back to the women, the dogs reluctantly followed. The first to ask what happened was Rachel. She noticed a small cut on John's hand. Without thinking she reached out and gently touched his hand, brushing off some sand. She placed a white handkerchief over the cut and poured water over it from her plastic water bottle.

As if suddenly aware of the others watching the delicate care, she was giving him, John thanked her and pulled his hand away. Rachel, a little surprised by his response, moved away from John and began walking toward the dogs that were running back and forth playing dog tag.

As tourists began filling in the empty spaces on the beach, the regulars turned and made their way back toward their homes. As John walked behind the group, he thought about Rachel's reaction to his small cut. Despite his denial, a smile swept across his face just for a second. However, one of the regulars saw it and she hid a smile as she turned back to the conversation buzzing around the group.

Rachel sat on her front porch and listened to the sounds her TV created as a backdrop against the over powering blackness of the quiet that usually filled her home. She wondered about John and remembered the warm feel of his hand and the rough calluses.

14

Pike was sitting on the steps to a private walkway leading to a summer home owned by someone who watched the movement of the ocean from afar. No one from the house seemed to ever venture out of the house to walk along the beach or dip their feet in the water.

Thankfully, no one ever came out of the house to shoo Pike away from the three steps at the end of the walkway. Every morning he walked the beach or sat and watched the sea gulls and pelicans. Every morning, weather permitting, John would walk his Brittany, Bud, along the wet sand of the waves that reached into the beach. Sometimes John waved at Pike as he passed. Few were the times that Pike responded in kind. Mr. Bud, always the ambassador of good will, would visit everyone who he met on his daily walks with his master.

Every morning Bud ran up to Pike, nuzzled him and made a pest of himself until Pike reached down and patted him on the head or, even better, scratched Bud's back. This made Bud and Pike friends forever or, so it was in Bud's head. Knowing that he had a standing assignment to find out more about Pike, John again changed his routine and followed his dog up to Pike.

As he walked toward Pike, Pike kept his head down, concentrating on Bud. When John was within ten feet, Pike lifted his head and made eye contact with John. "What's your dog's name?" said Pike.

"Bud is his name; sorry if he's bothering you," he said in his most pleasant voice. Both men remained silent, John shifted from one leg to another and Pike sat on the step keeping his eyes glued to the ocean in front of him. After a while John called to Bud and they turned to resume their walk. "Nice dog," muttered Pike from the steps as John turned to leave. "Thanks," John said over his shoulder as he continued to walk back to the tide line in the sand and complete his morning walk with Bud. A small smile slipped across John's face as he walked away from Pike. He knew how he was eventually going to cultivate a conversation with him Bud would be his ambassador.

15

As Pike made his way along the beach, he noticed a woman standing outside a house behind a half buried white picket fence. She stood clutching a beautiful shawl and staring out to the ocean. As Pike watched her, it was as if she could see something he could not. He stood staring for a few moments.

She turned and walked up the steps to her porch. With one hand on the door, she turned and looked in his direction. He turned away and put his head down, pretending to study something in the sand. As Pike stood looking at the sand at his feet, a chill swept down his back creating an unexpected shiver.

Moving down the beach, he studied the house he'd rented for the summer. He noticed some things he was supposed to take care of while his friend traveled the world with Julie. The paint, once a strong white with black trim, had faded from the beating of the salt air and the relentless summer sun.

As John walked back to his house later in the evening, he realized he had begun to understand this stranger who arrived on the island to find peace or even find himself. Pike would not be the first nor the last to find themselves on long stretches of beach and endless ocean that crept out to kiss the distant horizon.

The next day the mid-morning sun had already reached its zenith in the sky and the heat was seeping into the interior of the house. The small window would soon lose its battle with the heat. Shedding his light jacket and switching into his writing shorts, Pike sat down at his new computer; he knew it would take some time to get used to it. He finally made the decision to get rid of his typewriter. Words that swirled around in his mind for many years were attempting to escape. Even with the words swirling around in his head, at times they would not cooperate and flow onto the computer screen sitting in front of him. Frustration took over his mind; the words and ideas retreated into their hiding place. Reaching out and shutting down the computer, he leaned back. With a dark screen, Pike felt better. At least the cursor was not blinking, waiting for something from him. Leaning back in his chair, which began to creak and moan, Pike was not sure. Had the creaking originated within him or the chair? Slowly he got up, walked to the porch, and stepped outside.

The midday heat hit and took his breath away. He pulled off his T-shirt, and strolled to the beach. He stepped into the cooling waters of the Atlantic. After a shallow dive into an approaching wave, he surfaced. Then he floated on his back, looking at the billowy white clouds floating lazily overhead. Lost in his thoughts Pike floated in the water for a while, cooling both his body and his mind. An image of her intruded on his momentary calm. With a body shake he wondered why thoughts of her had come back after all these years? The question was still not answered. Why had he not been able to let her go? There had been other women in his life. Even some he had loved, whose memories now rested in a comfortable area of his brain. Unlike memories of her, which seemed to break into his thoughts of their own will, other memories seemed to resurrect at his bidding. Forcibly returning to the present, he stood up, walked to the shore, and back to his house. The combination of his frustration with his writing and the intrusion of her image led him to the hanging hammock on the porch. Gently balancing himself in the old army green tarp hammock, he closed his eyes. The gentle breeze from the ocean moved him back and forth. The night before, he had suffered a sleepless night, but now his eyes closed, and a soft snoring escaped his sleeping form. There was a last thought that tumbled around in his mind before sleep overtook him. He clenched his fists as the image of Maggie standing in front of the gym at Bolton College, waved at him across his mind's eye.

16

With the sun creeping over the horizon, the regulars gathered on the beach with their dogs. The dogs ran around, jumping, barking, sniffing. Each greeted one another, as if they had not been together in years, rather than just yesterday morning. The energy of the dogs was contagious. Carrying their morning beverage of choice, the regulars made their way along the beach. The conversation, like the dogs, was a way for members to greet and catch up on the latest. Strolling along the beach, they separated into small groups defined long before the summer began and not changing.

Suddenly, the group stopped. All eyes focused on John. They gathered around him, firing questions. John had a sudden image of General Custer at little Big Horn as the questions came at him from all directions. It was not difficult to determine the chief in this skirmish; it was Rachel. What more do you know about him? Who is he, what is he doing here?" Stepping back, John took a deep breath.

Choosing his words carefully, John told of his encounter with Pike yesterday morning if you could call it that. He looked at his gathered friends, each with a different facial expression.

Rachel stood behind the others, smugly smiling. Clearing his throat, John slowly explained it had been his dog, Mr. Bud, who was adept at introducing the possibility of an acquaintance. John closed his eyes, recreating the scene in his mind, before describing his encounter with the stranger.

Mr. Bud sat on the sand next to John and nudged his arm until John acknowledged him and scratched behind his ears. "He never talked to me or even acknowledged my presence. Bud had separated from me, as I was walking along the beach yesterday morning. Something about the man sitting alone on the carcass of a tree washed up on shore many years ago caught Bud's attention. Before he noticed it, Bud was on a steady path to the stranger. Uncharacteristically, Bud walked up to him and sat at his feet just staring. The man tried to ignore the dog, staring down at his book. But if you know nothing else about dogs, you must admit they can be patient.

Finally, the stranger put his hand down and let Bud smell. Then, the stranger started rubbing Bud just behind his ears. Well, that's all it took for Bud and the stranger to become friends.

After a few minutes Bud and I turned and walked toward the beach.

"As we walked away, I heard him say in a hoarse voice, 'Nice dog. Now you know what I know,'" John said, "and that was my introduction to the mysterious stranger." The others murmured on as they continued down the beach.

A couple days later, Pike stood and considered the work he needed to finish before the summer ended and his friend returned. As he thought about the needed work, he felt something pushing against his leg. Looking down he realized it was Bud, John's dog, again giving him the once-over. Pike reached down to scratch Buddy's ears. Looking up, he saw John coming his way. John's old baseball cap was pulled down over his eyes, attempting to block out some of the sun. Without waiting for an acknowledgement, John said, "I have a ladder." It was not the first time John knew what Pike was thinking before he had a chance to express his thoughts.

The day moved along as John and Pike worked together repainting the cottage. A friendship developed between the two men as they shared stories of their lives, talked about their dreams and the experiences that had brought them to this place at this time. As it is with men working on projects together, it created a bond and an opportunity to talk.

By the end of the day, the cottage had two sides freshly painted. Another side was primed and ready for the final coat. John and Pike finished the day with dinner at the local fish house, accompanied by drinks and laughter.

A week passed. One morning, the pelicans were extra diligent with their morning routine, swooping into the ocean after fish for breakfast as the regulars walked chatting.

Off in the distance on top of a driftwood log was the lone figure with his eyes focused on something out in the water. John knew before he could clearly identify the figure: it was Pike. As the regulars moved toward Pike, Bud shot off in a direct line toward him. John moved forward, yelling for Bud to stop, then realized Bud was on a mission. John also knew once Bud was on a mission, nothing would deter him, in this case, Pike.

John kept calling Bud, but the dog ignored him, moving as fast as his legs could carry him Finally, John reached the spot where Pike and Bud were eyeing each other in guarded caution; John was surprised at Bud's reaction.

The relationship between the two was suddenly changing. Slowly, with head bent low, Bud moved toward Pike, begging. Then, Bud sniffed Pike's pants pocket. Ears up, body moving with excitement usually reserved for something special. Bud was on full alert or as much of an alert as a senior dog can be. With deliberation, Pike pulled out a square of cheese. Mr. Bud moved forward with the same slow deliberate pace as Pike. If dogs can smile, then Bud was all smiles. From nowhere, all the dogs of the regulars surrounded Bud, reclaiming him as one of their own. Looking at Pike, John smiled and thanked him for the dog snack.

Two thoughts: one, Bud did not even seem to chew the snack and, two, Pike was definitely not as much of a loner as he had made folks think. Some people work at being loners and there are others for whom aloneness just comes naturally. Pike was not someone who had to work at being a loner; at least that is what John surmised after meeting him, helping him paint the cottage, and eating together.

17

The sun just began its journey back to the horizon when John decided to take a walk to clear his mind. He removed his sandals and let the cool wet sand of the incoming tide caress his aching feet. With sandals slung over his shoulder and a wide-brimmed hat pulled low over his eyes, John became lost in his thoughts. Her image, slowly appearing in his mind's eye, seemed to direct his footsteps; he had arrived back at her house or really his house rented to her for the summer.

Looking up, John saw a figure dressed in a man's white shirt and white shorts sitting on the steps of his rental house. As he moved closer, he saw the white shirt and the worn shorts with an array of colors spread out in an almost abstract design. With a shy wave of her hand, she looked and smiled that smile that engaged all parts of her face at the same time. Her brown eyes took his breath away for the second time that day as they caught the sun, or they just reflected something inside of her that John could not explain. Turning toward the faded white fence doing battle with the ever-advancing sand, John made his way toward the front porch. As he looked up at his house, he realized the old clapboards were struggling to hold onto their paint. Next summer he would tackle that job. Although that had been his plan for this summer, with a shrug, he dismissed the idea.As John got closer to Maggie, he knew she was out of his league. What was it about her that made him feel like a teenager again? It was the same feeling he sensed when he first met her as a prospective renter. "John, would you like some iced tea? You look warm." As she spoke, she stopped walking down the steps of the screened porch. Finding his voice, which seemed tight and tense, he said,

"Yeah, sounds great, but only if you are having some...." "John, come in out of the sun. I'll get the tea."

Looking around, John was astonished at how she transformed the porch in a few short weeks. Standing on an easel in the corner was a scene captured from an area up the beach. Not yet finished, its beauty was still evident. Then John noticed as he looked around the porch many canvases covered in scenes, but none of them finished. Even a couple of paintings with wet paint smeared on them.

Studying the various canvases, the feeling jumping out at him was frustration. There seemed to be a sharp contrast between the subject of the paintings depicting such peaceful scenes and the anger or frustration of the paint plastered against some of them.

Maggie returned with the iced tea. When she saw John studying her paintings, her smile disappeared, and air seemed to go out of the room. She led John back off the porch to the outside steps

Sitting down, she sipped her tea. "John, what brings you out this way?" Her voice was soft and smooth as it flowed from her lips. John held his glass up to his lips, not knowing what to do next. Looking up from his glass, he noticed she was watching him, her eyes soft and inviting. With a start, a realization hit him; she was waiting for an answer to something she had asked. Reaching back into his short-term memory, he searched desperately for some clue as to what she had asked him. It was no use. He would have to ask her for a repeat.

John awkwardly shifted his weight on the steps, trying not to moan as his old bones complained about having to sit on the stairs. Smiling, she looked at him and asked again what had brought him out this way this morning? John finally produced a reasonable explanation, hiding the fact he had hoped he would see her out on the beach. Looking at her and then turning away, he told her he was thinking of painting the north side of the rental house and wanted to take another look at it. She smiled and sipped her tea.

"Your paintings are beautiful," John said. Something had changed in Maggie's countenance. It was as if a cloud had descended over her and part of it was reaching out to cover John. "I don't want to talk about my paintings. My art brushes and I are not friends right now." Maggie lacked the usual smile in her voice, now more like that of a small child hiding behind her mother's dress in the presence of strangers. John realized this was not the time to ask questions. Finishing his tea, he stood and said goodbye, and began his journey down the beach. Looking back over his shoulder, he saw that Maggie had disappeared. John filed away in his memory her reaction when he had commented on her paintings. Reaching his house, he walked inside but was not able to forget the images that he had seen in Maggie's paintings. The images of her would linger in his mind for a while. Her eyes seemed incredibly sad. Something inside was haunting her. John decided to introduce her to the regulars. The early morning walks may help her find her a bit of joy again and find peace with her paint brushes.

18

As Maggie stepped out onto her porch, the first thing she noticed was the sound of dogs barking in the distance. The barking was not one of hostility or fear, but more like dogs playing. She watched the pelicans as they soared a few feet above the waves. They held their wings back and dove into the waves. After a few minutes, one would resurface with a fish in its beak. Repeatedly they soared and dove into the water. Maggie noticed the pelican's ungraceful appearance would suddenly transform before her eyes into a graceful work of art. For a moment, the desire to paint stirred her soul. The barking came closer and distracted her. It was the dogs she noticed first, as they came running around the fence between her and the beach. They should not have startled her; she'd seen them many times. They ran around and around each other and then dashed into the waves in an elaborate game likely developed centuries ago. Sometimes, when they glimpsed the sea gulls walking along the water line of the beach looking for food, the dogs would give chase. Then the sea gulls would squawk and leap into the sky amidst a flurry of feathers and wings as they left the dogs nipping at their feet.

Following close behind the dogs was that small band of people, ranging in age from about forty to early sixties. Some walked in small groups, others seemed to follow their own path, yet ever mindful of the group.

Following the dogs, to her surprise the group seemed to be heading in her direction, away from the water toward her house. As they drew closer she heard talking mixed with a rich blend of laughter. Maggie noticed a tall man leading the group, wearing an old slouch hat pulled down over his ears casting a dark shadow over his eyes. His beard that once perhaps was deep brown, now sprinkled with gray flecks creating an image of a man in transition from youth to another stage of life. His voice rose above the others as he waved and called Maggie by name. Caught off guard, foolishly she gave a small imperceptible movement of her hand. It was John.

The group stopped in front of Maggie's gate observing her. She searched each face in the group only recognizing John's face. She stood on her steps watching the group circle around her gate. It was his laugh made her grin a little. With exaggerated gestures, he waved at her.

"Maggie, come join us for a walk this morning."

From the back of the group, Rachel observed Maggie and John. What she learned from the two of them, she would file in her long-term memory to use at some other time and place. It was Rachel's voice that broke the silence of the moment,

"Maybe she does not want to walk with us this morning," Rachel said, with the confidence of someone who had a group of people behind her. There was a slight murmuring of the group as they looked to Maggie for a response.

It was Mr. Bud who convinced Maggie to join the group that morning. The small Brittany spaniel separated himself from the other dogs and made his way to Maggie. As he looked up at her with his soft brown eyes, Maggie melted and fell in love. Bending down she reached out and stroked Mr. Bud's head. He tilted his head back and gave her a lapping and a kiss. Something inside of Maggie connected with this dog standing in front of her. It seemed to touch the pain residing in her heart. She turned her attention back to the group and to John who was speaking. John made quick introductions round the group. Everyone reacted as if they had never heard of Maggie, even though John had talked for a few weeks now about the woman renting his cottage. Each of them knew about her from John's non-stop talk about her and her artwork, but they pretended they were hearing about her for the first time.

A spark seemed to ignite between Rachel and Maggie. It was something each of them was aware of as they stood sizing each other up. Rachel was wondering how Maggie would fit in, and if she would be a threat to her place in the group. For the first time in a long time Rachel felt defensive. Rachel watched John introducing Maggie to the group. He was more animated than usual and all his attention was on her. Rachel felt she needed to pull the group back to herself. She sensed something was about to change if she did not act. It was not long before Rachel asked the question, they all were waiting to hear... Rachel cleared her throat, which she had a habit of doing before she launched into a barrage of questions. Everyone knew when Rachel cleared her throat, the questions which followed either elicited information or answers.

Some of the regulars, broke eye contact and focused their gaze on the sand beneath their feet. There was an unusual tension. The women knew what it was. However, the men were clueless.

Rachel stepped toward Maggie, and looked her straight in the eye,

"So, what brings you to Pelican Island?" The question was asked with a chill the other women could touch.Rachel was looking directly into Maggie's eyes.

"Escape... from the noise of the city," she said, with an equal measure of chill just below the surface. Maggie locked her gaze on Rachel and refused to be the first to break eye contact. Rachel then did something no one had ever seen her do... she stepped back. Rachel recovered a bit and took a small step toward Maggie, sensing everyone was watching the interplay. With a voice that seemed to have lost some of its usual authority Rachel said,

"John tells us that you are an artist."Maggie shot a quick glance at John; he shifted his weight from one foot to other. Maggie looked at the group before she replied,

"Yes, I used to be an artist; now I am not." Attempting to reclaim the moment, John urged the group to continue their walk. Maggie thanked them for stopping by her cottage, but said she had to do some things around the house. With a promise to join them on another morning, she turned and walked back into her house.

Once inside, Maggie sat down at the harvest table in the small room on the back of the house she used as an office. She reviewed the morning's encounter with the "regulars" as John described them. Rachel was clearly the ringleader and had asked the questions the others had wanted to ask or had discussed, and Rachel was the chosen one to ask. The question seemed to reverberate in her mind, why had she come to this place after all these years? It was a question that Maggie would ask herself many times in the next few weeks.

Stepping into the kitchen Maggie brewed green tea and sat down on the brown Queen Anne's chair, she had found at a flea market the first day that she arrived on Pelican's Island. It felt comfortable as she sank into its arms and sipped her tea. The sound of the ocean and the sea breeze soon did their magic and she fell asleep in the old chair. Sleep came silently and let her escape for a little while. The face of Rachel and the stranger on the beach visited her dreams as she drifted away from the present.

19

With a promise of a new day, the sun crept up over a space between the Atlantic Ocean and the horizon. Maggie opened her eyes, slowly stretched her arms over her head, tousled her hair, wrapped a faded blue robe around herself and headed for the shower. In the shower, the cobwebs within her mind slowly cleared. She almost felt as if she was washing away her yesterdays and leaving room for a new day. She'd set the coffee timer yesterday and the smell of fresh coffee emanating from the kitchen drew Maggie toward it.

Fortified with the warm shower and coffee, Maggie walked out onto her porch. The unexpected dogs barking outside her cottage caused Maggie to flinch, and she spilled a few drops on the floor. Maggie looked through her porch windows as the regulars gathered around her picket fence.

Thinking about yesterday's meeting, Maggie surmised she had passed a test. Still, it felt like there was a cold hand on her shoulders and she shuddered. Who was Rachel, and why did she not want her in the group? Maggie sensed a competition brewing between her and that woman, but she could not figure out what the competition was or how it involved her. Brushing her hair back over her ear, she let go of the anxiety she had felt from yesterday's encounter.

Maggie stepped off her porch and joined the group as they made their way down the beach. Conversation developed easily as if it had replayed repeatedly. As with many groups, there were the talkers and the listeners. Rachel and John were talkers. John spoke softly, and the group seemed to listen when he spoke. Rachel's shrill voice was a bit pushy. John maneuvered through the group until he was standing next to Maggie. The closer he came to her, the more intense the look from Rachel. Maggie made eye contact with Rachel, who turned away to focus on the waves and the pelicans. Maggie became quiet and retreated into some other part of herself.

As Maggie watched John interact warmly toward each member of the group, she learned something about the man who had rented her his cottage. Despite his size and scruffy appearance, there seemed to be a big heart hidden inside, even gentleness drawing others to him. That must be why she felt so relaxed from the first day they had talked on the phone about renting his cottage. With a flash, another face popped into her mind, a face from long ago. A man, more of a boy at that time, with the same gentleness she now saw in John.

The dogs, already on to another adventure, ran up the beach, splashing in the waves and chasing each other. Tails wagged and barking continued as they glided along the beach. The regulars resumed their walk, taking time to remove sneakers or sandals, stepping into the cool incoming tide. They walked in a zigzag path, dancing with the waves of the incoming tide. Maggie soon realized one of the group's purposes was to discuss politics along with the gossip of the day.

Maggie figured she had been the subject of conversations before being invited to join the group. Groups' roles solidified over time and seldom did the positions change except possibly with the addition of a new member. However, for gossip there was no one better than Rachel, who knew something about everyone living on the beach. No one knew where she got her information, but it was usually true.

Rachel was the first to notice him sitting on the driftwood log. Her voice lost some of it shrillness as she pointed at the figure sitting on the log, "John, isn't that him?"

The regulars turned their attention to a man sitting on a log, writing, who seemed oblivious of the walkers passing by. John looked up and said,

"Yes, that's the man Bud ran up to yesterday." As if on some cue, from the pack of dogs, Mr. Bud ran toward the man. Rachel's voice once again broke the silence,

"John, what have you learned about him?" John stopped and turned to Rachel.

"I know he's a good house painter. He and I spent yesterday painting Tony's cottage which he's housesitting for the summer. I found out that he and I read the same mystery books by Cussler. We ended up going for dinner at Vinnie's Lobster House. He said he was interested in writing."

Maggie and Sandy, another woman from the group, stopped to collect sand dollars. As Maggie examined a sand dollar in her hand, she remembered collecting them with Julie, and the great conversations they had when they visited the island during spring break in college.

Maggie looked up at the group further down the beach. Bud came racing over the sand toward her, jumped up, and knocked Maggie on her butt into the water. She stood up, and brushed some the wet sand off her shorts.

She decided to head home and get into some dry clothes.

Maggie sat on her front porch early the next morning. The clouds sailed from north to south. Maggie took a deep long breath. The air was calm, however, there was the smell of a storm brewing. The sounds of dogs interrupted her thoughts. The regulars were walking toward her house, some with windbreakers, others carrying umbrellas of varied sizes and colors. John stopped in front of her porch, Good morning, Maggie." There was a small chorus as the other regulars wished her a good morning. Rachel moved over closer to John as Maggie stepped up from her rocker and invited the regulars onto her porch.

The rain came quickly, first small drops, then an avalanche of rain pellets. The regulars huddled together on the porch as the rain grew in intensity.

"Come inside," Maggie said, opening the door to her cottage. Everyone squeezed into her living room. She offered iced tea, but most had their own coffee or tea.

Thunder and then lightning struck with a resounding crack. The dogs paced the porch, attempting to hide from the storm as it attacked the shoreline. Maggie opened the door and the dogs searched for their masters. Some sat.

As quickly as the storm came in, it moved away. Slowly the clouds gave way to the sun. Most voted to continue their walk. A couple of the regulars seemed captivated by Maggie's artwork.

Rachel stood next to a canvas with a painting of the outcrop of rocks down the beach. She stood looking at the painting as the others filed out the door and onto the wet sand.

"Did you paint this?" Rachel asked. "This is amazing, the detail and the subtle shades of color among the rocks."

Maggie stepped up next to Rachel, "This is my peaceful area. The rocks seemed to suggest something without end as they stretch out into the sea. Thank you."

"I like it," said Rachel, and with that she turned and walked outside. The storm actually made Maggie feel a bit closer to the group.

Up ahead of them a man was walking in the water along the beach. He seemed to be walking with his head down looking for something. He was wearing a tan slouch hat and a blue windbreaker and black shorts that fell just above his knees. He had a backpack slung over his left shoulder.

The regulars stopped walking and watched the man. He stopped walking and bent over and picked up something out of the sand. Holding it up against the morning sun he examined it. With the fingers of his right hand, he slowly brushed the sand off the object in his hand. Pulling his backpack around he placed the object into a pocket in the backpack. Rubbing his hands together he brushed the sand from his hands. Turning he headed away from the water toward the Do Drop a small bakery.

The regulars continued their walk.

Rachel puffed out her chest, cleared her throat, turned to the group,

"Well, John said he is a writer, or at least he used to be. His name is Pike? What kind of name is that? He must have said Mike."

It was Maggie who reacted first. With a great intake of air, her stomach tightened. A gasp from somewhere inside of her caught the attention of the group. The group, as if on cue, stopped talking.

Maggie's response was not lost on Rachel, but then John had said it was most likely Mike. Maggie relaxed a bit. Rachel chose to let it go and use the information later at a better time. Maggie glanced over at Rachel and noticed a little smile at the corner of her lips. It only lasted for a split second, and then, it was gone.

John went off to retrieve his dog. Pike smiled as he scratched Bud behind his ears. If dogs could smile, there would have been a smile on Bud's face. Bud laid down in the sand at Pike's feet, waiting, watching. Pike pulled out a dog treat from his pocket. The sounds of Bud chomping on his treat from Pike made John smile. Pike looked up as John approached, "Like I said, nice dog." John smiled as he thought about how smart Bud was, and the cookie explained how the relationship between Pike and Bud developed so quickly. Dog treats from Pike created a great friendship between Pike and John's dog.

Each man felt the uneasiness of the moment. They sat in silence. It was Bud, who once again broke the barrier between the two men. Bud walked over to John, pushed his head up against John's elbow. Bud was anxious to get back with his friends, running around playing tag with the squawking sea gulls on the beach.

"In the sun, the paint on the cottage looks clean and bright," John said. "There is still the porch to paint; I can help you."

Pike murmured a thank you. John pulled Bud away by the collar and headed back to the group standing down by the incoming tide. They all seemed to be looking somewhere else, however, Rachel was standing staring straight at John and the new guy.

The next day the sun broke through the clouds early with the promise of a warm day. As the sun claimed more of the sky, the group settled into an easy pace both in their walking and their conversation. Being new to the group, Maggie had not heard them say much about the stranger.

The questions kept repeating themselves in Maggie's head as she listened to the others. Ever since a few days ago when she first noticed the man walking on the beach at dusk, something had stirred inside of her.

Who was that guy? She had seen him other evenings. The questions kept repeating inside her head. Whenever he saw her in the distance, he stopped whatever he was doing and watched. When she looked back, he averted his eyes. Did he know her? or had she met him? He looked familiar but she couldn't make the connection. All the women turned in unison and stared at Maggie. It was then that she realized that some of the thoughts that had been running through her mind had flowed out of her mouth for all to hear.

Rachel was the first to break the silence. "Do you know him?"

Regaining her composure, Maggie said

"No, the only person that I know is John. As you know, I'm renting his cottage for the summer."

Even if she did finally recognize the guy sitting on the beach, she was not going to share that information. The question was one that Maggie had asked herself just the other day when she was out walking and had seen him walking in the distance ahead of her. There was something familiar about him.It was his walk or something about the way he carried himself.

20

"John, where have you been? We haven't seen you this week for our morning walks." Rachel's voice was soft and encouraging as she spoke. The others in the group noticed the change in Rachel. John looked across the group at Rachel, who was smiling.

"Sorry about the morning walks. I have been sleeping in late the last few days." John knew his excuse was not going to satisfy Rachel for long.

John started walking forward along the beach and the others followed. There were no more questions from Rachel, which surprised him and the others.

John and Pike met again in the bakery shop on the beach just before sunset. They sat at a small table outside the shop, sharing stories.

Pike let down his guard and read a couple of poems he had written. John was amazed at Pike's ability to capture nuances in a scene.

A few days later, while John and Pike were again sitting outside the bakery. Rachel and her cousin, Susan, stepped onto the deck in front of the shop. Rachel's eyes grew big as she stopped in front of their table.

"Hi, John. Fancy meeting you here." It was impossible for John not to notice the dripping sarcasm in her words.

Before Rachel could say another word, John introduced Pike as a friend of Tony and Julie.

"He's staying in their cottage for the summer," he said, hoping the information would be enough to placate her for a while. John knew he would have a visitor later.

After leaving the shop and loitering about the shops, John walked to his home. Seated on the steps was Rachel, drinking a glass of wine.

"Do you have enough wine for two?" he asked, as he opened the door to his porch.

"Enough to share." Rachel stood up and stepped onto the porch. She sat down in her rocker, or at least it was the rocker she always sat in when visiting John.

John poured a glass for himself and refilled Rachel's glass. For a while they sipped their wine and listened to the sounds of the ocean.

"Well, I understand you've made a new friend in Pike, but we miss you on our morning walks." Her voice was soft and mellow. Maybe it was from the wine. Whatever the reason, John wasn't sure what to make of it.

"John, what is it between you and me?" She did not look at him but held her wine glass to her lips, appearing scared and anxious at the same time.

He took his time before he said anything. It was something he had been thinking about lately.

"I don't know, you are the most infuriating, opinionated woman I have ever known. You are also the most interesting person I ever met." John's words flew out of his mouth as he looked down at his sandals. "You are the only one who has ever challenged me like you do." His words were each chosen with great care. They seemed to originate from some deep struggle in his brain.

Rachel took a sip of wine, and faced John. "Me too." Her voice was just above a whisper.

They sat back in their rockers in silence.

The wine bottle was empty. John turned to Rachel, "May I walk you home?"

She nodded her head. They walked in the wet sand, splashing a little as each wave came in.

21

The regulars met outside Maggie's gate later than usual. The sun was already high in the sky. Maggie stepped down from her porch and joined the group. Rachel was the last to acknowledge her.

Tension within the group between Rachel and Maggie, and between John and Rachel, caused a few group members to think about leaving the morning walks. It all started when Maggie joined the group. Maggie seemed bewildered by the energy that seemed to exist between them. Maggie decided to give a quick excuse and not join them.

As she got closer to the group, she noticed John was not with them. John always made her feel welcome. Making a quick excuse, Maggie made her way back to the shelter of her cottage. She stepped onto the porch, glancing at the canvas in the corner of the porch. Sitting in front of her easel, she picked up where she'd left off the night before. The paintbrush had a mind of its own as it flew across the canvas. The stored creativity within her brain pushed everything else away.

An image had appeared in her mind in the middle of a restless night. Now the push to paint was stronger than the pull to sleep. Caffeine kept her energy high as she focused on the canvas in front of her.

It had been a long time since the desire to paint had been so strong. She let her mind soar. It became one with the brush. The man's shirt bore evidence of her work throughout the night. An image began to appear on the canvas, filling in the white spaces which had plagued her the last few months.

She smiled as she studied her work and her muse smiled for the first time in months. She wiggled the fingers of her left hand to relieve the cramping.

A knock at the door interrupted her thoughts. She closed her eyes and shook her head, "NO...NOT NOW!" The knocking persisted, "Maggie, its John, are you in there?" Her muse shook her head and shouted, "NO, DON'T STOP!!"

She could see his shadow through the screen door. With one look, he realized he had interrupted something important. Her shirt was covered with paint splatter. There were dried specks of paint on her face. Dark circles gathered under her eyes, her hair was pulled up in a tangle.

"You are painting!" As soon as he said it, he realized how stupid it must sound. There were the weeks of listening to her talk about having been a painter, but no more. He realized how important this moment was for her. Turning on the porch, he figured it was time to leave, but struggled to make an inroad into Maggie's world.

"How about dinner tonight? You will need to eat sometime today." But he knew the one date they had was also the last.

Maggie was off limits. There was a sadness within her; he was not going to be the one to fix it. He knew from experience it was time to retreat and give up the fight.

She put down her paint brush, and turned to face John, as he put his hand on the door of the porch.

"John, we can be friends, but it cannot be any more than that," said Maggie. "You're a good friend and I would hate to lose that."

Once again, she'd declined his invitation and

re-established the boundaries of their friendship. They would be friends and nothing more. "We can be friends," he said. "I don't want to lose that." He did not turn away from the door as he spoke. "See you for the early morning walk on the beach tomorrow."

For some reason, he thought of Rachel. With a shrug, he erased her image. She was not likely going to someone really important in his life. A shudder swept through his body. Her image brought mixed emotions.

Maggie returned to her painting and the muse returned in full force. Once again, the image appeared in her head and the paint began to cover the vacant white areas of her canvas. She stood in front of the easel and disappeared into her painting as the outside world faded away.

Climbing the steps to his porch, John sat down in his rocker. Looking out at the rolling waves marching toward the beach then retreat into the sea, John settled back into the arms of his chair and let his mind drift for a moment. A minute turned into an hour. The warmth of the sun reached out and caressed him as he rocked.

With the slowness of a man lost in thought, John put his hands on the well-worn arms of his chair and pushed himself to a standing position. Opening the screen door, he decided to change clothes, put on new shorts instead of his work clothes and take a walk along the beach. The lateness of the day told him the regulars would all be home having lunch and not appear again until the sun was starting to set.

As he made his way out the door, right behind him was Mr. Bud, making sure to not be left behind. Usually when something was on his mind, John just walked the beach, losing himself in his thought, oblivious to what was going on around him. Friends had remarked seeing John walking aimlessly along the beach, so lost in his thoughts he did not acknowledge their presence when they passed on the beach. Close friends of Johns would not take it personally, knowing he was trying to work something out in his head. It could be a problem he was having in his workshop or something more serious, such as thoughts of his late wife who had fought valiantly against cancer but had died three years earlier. The wound was still healing and the John everybody cared about was returning.

As was the case, sometimes a short walk along the beach

became an extended sojourn through the midday and into the beginning of the early evening.

About five in the afternoon, John realized he had ended up in front of Rachel's house, where she sat on her covered porch. He could see her drinking something.

"Well don't just stand there. Come on up and have some iced tea just made it." Rachel said, getting up from her chair. John remembered later her voice had not been shrill but softer and more inviting. As they sat sharing drinks, they talked. He later said, when asked about that day, he felt calm sitting at the table with her.

22

Maggie began the day early, considering she had been up late painting. For the first time in a while, the urge to paint was stronger than the voice critiquing her work. The muse's voice sometimes was so loud she expected those around her to hear it. It used to be a mere whisper as she painted, now it was a constant roar. Maggie thought early mornings the best time to paint. The muse was not an early riser.

She slipped into her paint splattered shorts and shirt.

After working for a couple of hours in the early morning, she was ready to get out of the house for some fresh air. Grabbing a snack bar, she kicked off her shoes, pushed open the screen door, and headed for the water. Her hair tied back in a ponytail, swung back and forth with her every step. She took a deep breath for the first time all morning. The water felt cold for a moment, then her body adjusted, and a feeling of peace replaced her stress.

Later, walking with her head down, she studied the movements of a small leathery starfish, caught in a backwater pool by the retreating tide. As she watched it struggle with the draining pool, she took pity on the little sea creature, picked it up and returned it to the sea. It moved away from its captivity and disappeared. She smiled as she thought about how lucky the starfish was to escape and return to its world.

Looking up, she realized someone was watching her. About a

hundred feet in front of her a man stood watching her. As she glanced at him, she felt something in her stomach tighten and a catch in her breath. There was something about him that felt strangely familiar.

She adjusted her sunglasses, and he came more into focus, but still he was standing with the sun behind him. She could not make out his facial features. A wide brimmed tan hat sat at an angle on his head, casting a shadow over his face. A close-cut gray flecked beard defined the edge of his face. The beard did not match images racing through her mind.

Pike had watched the woman step into the water, bend over, and set the starfish free from its sand prison. The soft sea breeze played with a few strands of brown hair. With her left hand she pushed the few strands behind her ear. A face crept into his mind, a face from long ago. He stood watching as she turned around and walked back down the beach.

It was not until he strolled into Tony and Julie's cottage that he realized who it might be. He sat down on the rocker on the porch and began to rock slowly back and forth. The pounding in his chest caused him to stop rocking.

He stood slowly and went back out to the beach. He searched for her, but she was gone. He stood in the water letting the small waves wash over his feet. Was it really Maggie? How did she get here?

He thought about Tony and Julie; did they know that she would be down here on the island when he was? Is that why Tony wanted him to stay in his cottage for the summer?

He walked along the smooth wet brown sand along the edge of the beach. There was no sign of her.

After almost a week of looking for her he returned to his driftwood log and began to write again in his journal. He watched the regulars as they paraded by in the early mornings.

Maggie sat on her porch looking at a blank white canvas daring her to fill it up. She grabbed a piece of soft charcoal from her wooden box her father gave her when she left for the summer on the beach. She slowly opened the box, all the chalk and charcoal sticks.

Maggie's hands raced over the canvas, the white spaces began to disappear, gray lines and shades of gray began to form an image. Maggie's memory and the stranger she saw earlier in the morning began to blend together.

She sat back and looked at the drawing of a man. The shadows of the tan hat and the posture of his body pulled emotions long ago tucked away.

Maggie stepped away from the drawing, turned and walked out the door of her cottage. She walked and walked, failing to escape the image on her canvas. The sun had set, and a cool breeze drifted in from the ocean.

The beach was hers and hers alone. She found herself at the rocks. She sat down and leaned her back against the warm rocks. Pulling her knees up to her chin, she let the memories from the past run through her mind.

"Pike, what are you doing here?" Her question seemed to just float out in front of her. "Pike, why now after all these years?" Resting her head on her knees, she just let the past anger and pain rush out into the empty space around her.

The sun had long since hidden behind the horizon and the breeze off the water turned chilly.

She walked home and went to bed early. The morning began with a steady rain followed by crackling lightning and the growl of thunder. Maggie rolled over in her bed as the cottage shook with the last bout of thunder. The lightning lit up the room, followed by the rumble of thunder.

Throwing the covers off, she made her way to the kitchen. The lights flickered, then came back on. Making coffee and reaching for a bran muffin she pondered yesterday morning. She walked out on the porch.

Wrapped in a blanket, she watched nature's fireworks in the sky. Counting the seconds between the thunder and lightning, she guessed the storm was right on Pelican Island. With each bout of lightning she pulled the blanket a little tighter around her shoulders.

The lights flickered then went out. A knocking on the door she jumped.

"Maggie, are you alright?" John's voice drifted in between the lightning and thunder display.

"John, come in."

He opened the door and formed a puddle inside the porch.

"I have an old-fashioned hurricane lantern. It's ancient but it works."

"Thanks, John. May I get you a muffin?"

"I never turn down a muffin," John said and laughed.

John turned up the wick on the lantern and then lit it. Its yellow light filled in some of the dark spaces on the porch.

"Sit down, John." Maggie was happy to have someone around during the storm. John took off his raincoat and hat and sat down in the other rocker. He rocked slowly, and his eyes slowly roamed around the porch and stopped at the drawing on the canvas in the corner. Maggie caught him staring at it.

He kept staring. It sure looked like Pike. However, the face was hidden in shadow.

Maggie's voice was tight. "Oh, it's just something I was scribbling with this morning."

John figured he would keep his thoughts to himself. Well, looks like it's clearing up," John said, standing up and looking out toward the ocean. The clouds were still racing across the sky, but not as dark as they were earlier. The thunder and lightning had stopped. The rain continued but had lost some of its fury.

John moved toward the door, putting his raincoat back on.

Maggie stood, "Thanks for coming over. I've hated thunder storms ever since I was a kid."

"If you need anything just let me know," John said as he put on his hat. The lights flickered and then returned.

"No walkers today," John said as he hurried down the steps.

―――◦《◉》◦―――

Pike knew. He had seen those eyes that pulled him toward her cautiously, that created a change in Pike's breathing. For an instant, he was again twenty years old and in college with the most beautiful girl he had ever known. Her deep brown eyes had not changed. They still had the same effect on him. The voice was more mature, but still the same.

Each of them began walking toward the other. The awkwardness of the years that had passed stepped in between them. Each held a load of memories slipping out from their time in college.

The break up so many years ago now seemed in the present. Memories locked away now caused each to take a step back. The words came slowly, hesitantly as they tried to control the memories rushing around in their brains.

Maggie was the first to break the wall of silence, growing thicker with each moment.

"Pike, is it you?" Maggie whispered, her voice hoarse as if she had been yelling all night. Pike felt like his voice seemed locked away somewhere. He smiled despite everything he was feeling. As seconds passed, neither of them noticed they had begun moving closer to each other.

The words came slowly, then in a rush, pouring forth explosively, both talking at the same time. Each one reaching out to touch something buried inside for decades.

"Maggie, would you like to meet for coffee?" Pike asked, hesitantly. He could feel his heart ready to explode. So many feelings rushed to the surface.

Maggie looked at Pike... searching for the boy that she once loved. She knew she should say no, and not stir up more feelings from her past.

"Yes," the word slipped out so softly, Pike was not sure if he'd heard right

He looked at her cautiously. "How about tomorrow?"

"Yes, that would be good, what time?"

They found a special little coffee house close to the beach. Pike impressed Maggie by remembering; she'd always liked hazelnut coffee with cream and no sugar. Their conversation started out light, remarks about Pelican Island, favorite cafes, fun with friends, new people to meet. But for some reason comments became stilted as neither one sensed the courage to dig back into the true questions—the confusion and pain of the past. Sometimes there comes a time in a conversation when each person knows it is time to end it.

As they walked out of the café in opposite directions, they thought about the good times they had in college, memories came back in a torrent, questions, why now after all these years? What happened to us? For each of them, different answers.

Maggie stopped walking; other memories of that time in her life came to the surface. HE CHEATED! She could not trust him. They had even started talking about getting married. He cheated. That phrase, like a phone that never stopped ringing, kept coming back to her repeatedly. Anger, pain, long since tucked away swept over her in a strong wave as she looked out over the unending beach in front of her. Maggie thought about the secret that she was holding back from Pike. He had a daughter that he never knew about. Pike was the father of Tasha. Maggie had the baby after Pike had left college. Maggie tried to find him but gave up. So many times, in the years that passed she wondered how he was doing and if he ever thought about her. She thought about Pike here and now how could she tell him about Tasha?

The secret she kept from Tasha and from Pike. It felt like a heavy burden that she had carried over the years. It was time to share the secret with Pike and Tasha. She thought about the possibility that neither one would talk with her after they found out. Maggie stopped walking, sat down in the warm sand in the early evening. She looked around; without realizing it, she was back at the rocks. The beach was empty, so was Maggie.

A tear not shed in a long time, slipped out from the corner of her eye, slid down her cheek. With a clenched fist, she wiped it away. Too many tears shed in the past. She decided not to show up the next day. If only it was as easy to wipe a tear as it was to wipe away a wounded heart.

Maggie leaned back against the rocks, pulled her knees up under her chin. She thought about the days after Pike left and she found out about being pregnant. She remembered the day that she told her parents and the anger her father had for Pike. Maggie's mother had tried to comfort her as her father kept pacing in the living room. She remembered her younger sister walking in on the conversation. Betsy, her nine-year-old sister had really liked Pike. She had been standing in the kitchen listening to the conversation between her mother and father and Maggie.

Without pausing Betsy barged into the room. "I hate Pike." Her words filled the room. Father stopped pacing, mother got up and put her arm around Betsy and pulled her to the couch. The family sat in silence. Maggie remembered crying, like she had let her family down.

Maggie was in shock, she thought about being a mother with a daughter and supporting her on her own. It was a challenging time; baby Tasha had the same eyes at Pike. It was hard to miss she went to her closet in her bedroom and pulled out the small red box on the top shelf. She would sit on her bed going through the love letters written by Pike and the picture of Pike, Tony, and Julie at the beach on Pelican Island. The smiles on the faces brought back many memories.

She watched her daughter grow into a strong young woman. The years were difficult, money was tight, eventually her family accepted Tasha as part of the family. Betsy became close with Tasha. She always said it was like having a younger sister.

Pike's name never mentioned. Tasha grew up without a truly loving father in her life. When Tasha became a high school student, she became more curious about who her father was. Maggie did not tell her. She told her it was somebody that she knew a long time ago.

Pike clenched his teeth as he walked back to his log on the beach. The good memories that accompanied him as he had started to walk away from Maggie seemed replaced by anger and pain. In a burst of empty laughter that came from somewhere inside he asked himself how she could still have such an effect on him. As he sat on his log watching the seagulls play tag with the tide, a memory of the end of the relationship came back. It was during their senior year and after spring break and graduation was fast approaching. There had been a lot of talk about getting married and the end of college. She already had found a job in an elementary school as an art teacher. She was happy and seemed to be moving away from him. The more he felt her moving away the more he thought about not wanting to be the one left behind.

The night before Christmas break, Maggie told him she hated being away from him for even a week. As far as she was concerned, Pike would never even flirt with other girls, no matter how beautiful or charming.

But the break up came just before graduation. It was painful, and both walked away thinking the other had lost interest. What neither one of them realized was that the decision would haunt them for the next thirty years. A broken heart may mend after thirty years but some scars on the inside, remain a reminder of something that could have been.

Pike had decided sometime in the early morning hours when sleep refused to come, he would not show up at the bakery shop. Why should he risk another occasion for Maggie to change her mind? The decision had the opposite effect on him. Instead of allowing him to fall asleep, it kept him tossing and turning until sunrise.

It was the regulars who noticed the differences. Maggie seemed cut off; she had decided not to join them for their early morning walks. John spent more time walking near Rachel. When they passed the place where Pike had been every morning with his coffee and writing journal, the log was empty. As usual, it was Rachel who broached the subject the others were thinking about.

"John, have you seen Pike?" Rachel's voice seemed softer this morning, lacking the usual harshness.

There seemed to be a change in the atmosphere of the group. Sandy, the quiet one, voiced the question that everyone else was thinking.

"What is going on? The group seems different today. Does anyone else feel it or is it just me?" The others turned like a band on a football field during homecoming. All eyes focused on Sandy. No one could remember her speaking more than two complete sentences in a row since they'd been roaming the beach.

John shifted uncomfortably from one foot to the other and made sure he did not catch Rachel's eye. She tried to break the silence that descended over the group.

Maggie paced back and forth in front of her easel trying to remember the purpose of her work. The muse seemed to hide from her or maybe she wasn't in the mood. Sleep did not come easily last night twisting, turning, she paced the porch searching for answers. Knowing the regulars had already passed by, she ventured out onto the beach and headed toward the water.

Stepping into the incoming tides, she felt relief. As the water touched her feet, the tension building all night drained into the water,

Of course, she knew what was killing her. It was running into Pike again and all the memories that came flooding back. Pike was the past: done with, filed away in a closet of her brain marked ancient memories.

She wrestled with two thoughts that seemed to be at war. One wanted to never see Pike again. Nothing he could say would change the past. The other part of her was screaming, "Maybe there's something he could say that would change things." The pain she remembered when she found out Pike had cheated on her was one of the worst times in her life. Shoving everything she had built up over the years, she pushed all the feelings and the anger back into the hole they came from.

Turning, she walked away from the usual path of the regulars toward another part of the beach. The area was where the "newbies" had built large mansions that changed the landscape and ruined the beach. At least that was what the regulars had told her repeatedly on the early morning walks. As she walked alone along the beach, she thought about the regulars and how she seemed to fit in with the group. They were an odd assortment of characters she had fallen in with. The conversation, the laughing, the beach was all better than her life in Chicago. For a moment she thought about what it would be like to stay at the beach.

23

The morning was overcast with a thick mist in the air. "Where did Maggie come from, and exactly why is she here at this time? Is it part of some ethereal plan or just a fluke?" Pike's voice grew silent.

He walked on, oblivious to the mist in the air. He thought about running into Maggie last week and the plans to meet for the second time. He had decided not to go.

Pike stopped walking. He wondered if Maggie had shown up at the coffee shop? He'd decided not to take the chance that she would show up.

He turned to face the ocean, the waves just kept coming like the thoughts in his mind. Images pulled from the past formed a collage of memories seemingly from another world.

He looked down the beach at Tony's cottage, so many times spent on the beach with Tony, Julie, and Maggie.

The last time he and Maggie had sat on the beach watching the fire they had built. Snuggling up on a log they'd spoken about the end of college approaching and the life they planned after college.

Maggie was so warm leaning against his body, all he could think of was spending the rest of his life with her.

Graduation was just around the corner, things would change. They had talked about getting married after graduation.

He started walking along the beach. The bakery was on the right just off the beach. There had been many a conversation about the future while sitting on the deck of the shop. Pike turned toward the Do Drop In and sat at a small table under the covered deck. He pulled out his notebook from his back pack. Slowly he pushed his pen across the page trying to make sense of his thoughts and feelings. The words, emotions, and images were a jumble moving around his mind.

He thought about the last day that he saw Maggie. It was the day after graduation. He had driven to her parent's house. She had come to the door. One more time he attempted to tell her how much he loved her. She never said anything. She simply put her hand on the door knob, turned and said, "I trusted you with my heart."

He never knew what she meant by that.

Pike rewound the moments of his senior year at Bolton. A face jumped into his mind. A long-haired blond girl with deep blue eyes. She had worked on the school literary journal. The two of them had worked a lot together.

Another image followed—again, it was Nancy, the blond fresh-man. It was a dorm room, not his. He sat staring at the image in his mind. She was smiling, and in bed. Pike kept looking at the image. He had gone to her dorm room one afternoon. She started kissing him as soon as they entered her room. She lay down on the bed.

He sat down on the bed. She slipped under the covers and started taking off her clothes.

"No, I can't do this," Pike said.

"Then why are you here?" she yelled

"She won't know," she whispered. "I love you, Pike."

Pike turned and walked out of the room. On his way down the hallway, Maggie's friend, Carol, said, "Pike, what are you doing here?"

Pike kept walking.

Pike left the dorm and went to his room for his history note-books and backpack. Tony sat in his room reading his business law book for his upcoming final exam. He had an A going into the final; he was not worried.

Pike stopped at the door to Tony's room. Tony looked up. Tony knew that Pike should never play poker; his face always gave away what he was thinking.

"Pike, what's up? Are you ready for your last final of college?"

Pike walked in and sat down on the bed.

"I did a real stupid thing this morning. I stopped in at Nancy's room to return some of the articles she asked for to finish a piece she was working on for the Bolton Literary Journal. When I walked in she hugged me and started kissing me." Pike explained the rest of the encounter with Nancy.

Tony closed his book. "Pike, what were you thinking?" Tony stopped, he knew Pike was hurting.

"Tony, I don't know what to do, should I tell Maggie?"

Tony sat watching his friend. "If you don't, someone else will, or Nancy will."

Pike left his dorm with so many things swirling around in his head. He opened the door to the library; all tables and chairs were filled with students studying for exams. Walking down the stairs to the lower level of the library, he saw Nancy with her back to him sitting with a bunch of her friends.

He made his way down the stacks to a far corner of the library. There was a small table and chair in the corner facing a window. He dropped his backpack on the table, pulled out his history book and his notebook. Arranging everything on the table he opened his book and began rereading the last chapter for the final. Putting on his reading glasses, he dove into his book.

The final exam was just days away and he needed a strong final exam to get a "B" in the class.

As Pike read his notes, his mind went back to the dorm room. The question that kept nagging his brain: do I tell Maggie? Like in a small town, there are no secrets in college.

Pike closed his book, and pushed everything into his backpack.

He was angry with himself for getting into the situation; he could not concentrate. What would Maggie think?

Looking up, he glimpsed the blond girl marching straight for him. She pulled out a chair across from him. Pike folded his arms across his chest, putting up a wall between him and Nancy.

"I feel dirty," she whispered. "Why did you leave?"

Pike just looked at her, "I'm sorry. I just couldn't."

She stood, turned, and stomped off. Reaching the first row of tables full of students studying for finals, she turned back to Pike.

"Stop following me around!" she yelled at Pike.

Pike stared at her. Other students stared at Pike. As they returned to their books, a few guys smiled, glad it was not them.

Pike turned and made his way to the coffee shop at the edge of the beach. The memory of that day in his senior year at college was one that still haunted him. It was so long ago, but sometimes it seemed like just yesterday. Shaking his head, he tried to erase the images in his head.

Pike stood up and ordered his usual cup and a sweet roll from Bennie the owner. Pike looked out at the rain replacing the mist of the earlier morning.

Pike returned to his table and began writing in his journal. The rain continued; he knew he would have to face the rain and Maggie.

Maggie awoke slowly, the pounding of the rain on the roof stirred her from a night full of images from another day. Sitting up, she stared at the pile of sheets and blankets, witness to her restless night. Pulling on her T-shirt, she made it to the shower. The hot water helped her wake up to face the day.

Fortified with a hot coffee and a couple of warm blueberry muffins, she opened the porch door. The rocker beckoned her from the corner of the porch. Biting into a muffin, she sorted through images and memories once locked away, now freed.

Running into Pike a couple of days ago had stirred forgotten things that she thought she'd locked safely away. Looking out at the beach, she remembered the great times she and Pike, Tony, and Julie spent in Tony's parent's cottage during spring breaks and a few weeks in the summer. Senior year was special. She thought about the bonfires at night, growing friendships, and fun experiences.

She thought about the last bonfire she and Pike shared during the last spring break, senior year. She and Pike were alone on the beach, snuggling together as the fire sent its sparks into the night air. The smell of the logs burning, melding with Pike's English Leather cologne created strong memories.

Maggie thought about Pike and her daughter, Tasha, whom he knew nothing about. Maggie stopped rocking and stood, looking at the ocean. It never changed; it just kept coming wave after wave.

Maggie thought about the last time she saw Pike after graduation. She never let him know why she broke up with him.

From the window in her bedroom, she watched him drive away. She felt like her world had just crashed. The months after college were difficult. She had Pike's baby but she did not know where he was.

Maggie and her baby, Tasha, moved out of her parent's house and moved into a small one-bedroom apartment near the college. She remembered how angry her father was that Maggie had a baby and no father. He was angry with Pike, who had been like a son to him.

Maggie got a job as a teacher; her mother took care of Tasha during the day. Maggie worked as a teacher for ten years and then started to sell her paintings. Eventually she quit teaching and sold her paintings in a small Chicago gallery.

Tasha eventually went off to college in a small town in Iowa. She and her mother seemed to distance themselves from each other. Tasha came home from college less often every year. There was a wall that grew stronger every year. Maggie tried to get close to Tasha, but she stayed away.

Maggie could not give Tasha the one thing that she wanted, a true father. Tasha became more insistent to know who her father was, but her mom never mentioned Pike's name.

During her senior year in college Tasha found a small packet with letters and one picture of a man with long hair and a dark beard.

At the end of her senior year Tasha confronted her mother about the man in the picture. Maggie said it was somebody she knew a long time ago.

Tasha looked at her mom, "Who is the guy in the picture; is he my father?"

Maggie shook her head, "It's just somebody that I knew during another time in my life." That was the last time Maggie talked with her daughter about the man in the picture.

Maggie and Tasha did not speak after that day. Tasha did not come home after college. She got a job around her college and stayed there.

Maggie shut down her heart concerning Pike after college and never reopened that closet. The other part of her heart was her daughter, Tasha. She had not seen her daughter in the last five years. Every year Maggie sent a postcard to Tasha. There was never any return card from her daughter.

Pike coming into her life stirred up a lot of memories. She thought she'd finally made peace with her past. She had decided not to show up the next day after meeting Pike for coffee. She was curious as to whether Pike had shown up.

Early the day after meeting Pike she did stroll by the coffee shop. She looked in from the beach. He was not there. Maggie was confused about how she felt. Part of her felt like it was easier to let go. Another part of her wanted to know about his life. Maggie's feelings, never resolved, were only buried.

Maggie did not join the regulars during the next few weeks.

John showed up one morning by himself. He stood at the steps to the porch.

"Maggie, are you in there?" his voice strong and full of confidence. "Maggie, it's John."

Maggie sat at her kitchen table reading. She looked up at the porch. She was not sure who was calling to her.

"Yes, John, good morning." She reached out and opened the door to her porch, "Come in, would you like some iced tea?"

"Yes, we haven't seen you for a while, wondering if you were alright?" John's voice was warm.

Maggie walked into her kitchen and returned with two plastic cups of iced tea. John was sitting in the far rocker, rocking back and forth slowly, gazing out the window. "Looks like it's going to be a beautiful day."

"Where have you been? We've missed you in the group."

"Maggie took a sip of her tea and turned to John, "I've been painting."

John looked around the porch; there was one blank canvas sitting on the easel. He decided not to mention it.

"Well, I hope you decide to come back to the group for morning walks. Rachel was asking about you the other day,"

"I'll be back, just needing some time to finish some projects."

Rachel said she saw you the other day talking with some man on the beach. You know Rachel; she never misses anything."

Maggie decided not to respond to that comment. "Well, John, what have you been up to?" Maggie said. She hoped that it would take John in a different direction.

"I've been working on a cradle for my neighbor's daughter. Sometime when you're free, stop by and look."

John knew when it was time to leave. He stood, finished the rest of his iced tea, and handed the cup to Maggie. "Well, I'll be getting back to the regulars, who should be just about starting out this morning. Sure, you don't want to join us?"

"No, not this morning, but soon." Maggie took the cup from John as he left the porch.

24

2010

Maggie and Pike had met again on a cold cloudy day in the first week of September, thirty years after their very first encounter as freshmen in college.

The early fall wind had changed its direction, coming strong off the Atlantic. White caps and threatening waves marched up the beach.

Maggie bundled up in an old Bolton College sweatshirt. She strolled with her head down, trying to block some of the blowing fine sand stinging her eyes. Finally giving up the walk on the beach with the wind and sand attacking her, she hurried back to the protection of her cottage.

Pike tossed and turned as the hours slipped slowly by. The window across from his bed was still dark. Even the sun was not ready to make its appearance. As Pike lay in his bed, his eyes wide open, a thousand thoughts ran through his mind. What was it that was bothering him? What was it about being with her again that kept gnawing at his brain. Something too unsettling.

Everything had seemed to go well with Maggie. Good conversation, residual affection, but... What was the *but* that kept intruding, especially in the early morning hours, when sleep just seemed to escape him.

With a long sigh, he turned over and closed his eyes, trying to turn off the voices in his head. Instead of much-needed sleep, he replayed the events of the last few weeks over and over in his mind.

Though in denial, Pike had noticed her the moment he glimpsed her in the group of regulars as they made their way along the beach with their cadre of dogs. She was not one of the regulars. However, he had noticed her the last few mornings. She seemed to walk a little separated from the group or usually with John. They seemed locked in conversation. She usually carried a walking stick and used it to probe things she found along the beach washed up by the tides.

It was her mannerisms that first caught Pike's attention, the smile, the way she walked. Later when they were closer, Pike recognized her laugh. It was a laugh coming from inside, infectious, capturing all those around her, making others feel a part of her circle. Her hair, now grayer than when he had known her, ran free to her shoulders.

Those memories came back so quickly, because Pike had never stopped thinking about her. For him recognition had been almost instant; Maggie was the woman he was seeing with the morning regulars.

The days and nights since Pike and Maggie's encounter the Pelican Island beach thirty years after college were a blur. Long phone conversations into the early morning, a thousand questions, memories from the earlier life and the years in between. He recalled midnight dinners shared with wine, only the stars watching as they sat on the beach listening to the never-ending rhythm of the waves.

Voices began to speak to Pike a whisper, then a roar in his ear night and day. *She left you before. She will leave you again.* At first, Pike ignored the voices and listened to his heart. The memories in his head were stronger than the new voices in his heart.

Soon doubt replaced the joy of just being together, sharing thoughts and feelings. The flaws and fears created a different tone with each of their voices. Gone, a chance to lose themselves in each other, oblivious to the world around them. It was the knot in Pike's stomach when the phone rang, or whenever he walked to her house to share some time together. The knot replaced feelings of connection and the healing of his heart.

It was late in the afternoon when Pike's phone rang. The knot in his stomach formed when he heard her voice on the phone.

"Pike can we meet later this afternoon?"

"What's up? I thought we were going to meet tomorrow morning." Pike listened carefully not just to the words but the tightness in Maggie's voice. Pike arrived early at the bakery, Maggie was already there sitting at a small table. There were two iced teas on the table. Pike sat down across from Maggie.

Maggie spoke the words both had been dreading. They caught in her mouth as she tried to speak. "Pike, oh, Pike," she whispered, as she sat across from him in the small coffee shop that had become their morning routine. Each was armed with their own favorite coffee. They sat across from each other, joining the customers who flowed during the early morning rush.

Looking at him, her eyes began to water. She brushed the tear forming in her eye, hoping Pike had not noticed, which was unlikely as he rarely missed anything.

"Maggie, are you ok? What's wrong?" he whispered, already knowing what it was.

She reached out and grabbed each of his hands. Pulling them forward, she raised them to her face and spoke behind their protection.

"I need to have some time away from us," she whispered between their fingers. Pike reached across the table and took Maggie's hands into his.

Pike's blue eyes widened abruptly, and he focused on her deep brown eyes. He could see her pain. He had figured this conversation was coming, but it did not make it easier.

"I know, Maggie, things are not perfect between us." With his words, Pike lowered his head and his eyes lost their intensity.

"We are overly critical of each other and cannot seem to agree on even what day of the week it is."

"Pike, I need to be by myself for a while." With each word her voice lost its softness and a hardness crept in.

Not a voice remembered from their college days but one showing itself only in the last few months.

"Pike, please do not call me. I will call you when I'm ready." With her words still hanging in the air she got up, grabbed her cup, and walked out the door.

Pike sat there, his gaze following her until she disappeared from his view. Slowly raising his cup to his lips, he jumped at the heat, spilling some coffee on the table. Knowing this conversation was coming had not made it easier. Just final.

As we all do, Pike sat at the table running mentally through the last few weeks—the times that he and Maggie had spent together after not seeing each other for thirty years. Sometimes the past was just too difficult to recapture. Maggie's words just seemed like a kick in the stomach, sucking all the air out of his lungs. He felt he had been holding his breath, or was only breathing in short shallow breaths. After refilling his cup, he made his way out of the coffee shop, turned, and took one last look around. It would not be the same tomorrow when he came for his morning coffee. She would not be there.

With tears in her eyes, Maggie walked away. Nothing she could do would stop this. An old man asked if she was ok. She forced a smile but failed miserably. He touched her elbow and whispered, "His loss."

Pike grabbed his thermos and backpack and rushed out the door. Last time she left he did not go after her, this time he would.

Rushing outside, he saw her standing, her back bent forward, her hands were covering her eyes. An old man was talking with her.

"Maggie!" Pike yelled and ran toward her.

The old man turned and walked toward Pike.

"She loves you but you got to give her some time."

Pike ignored the old man and caught up with Maggie.

"Is this really what you want, Maggie? Are you going to just run away after all these years?"

"Pike, I love you. I just need a little more time."

"Maggie, I love you too. Just please don't run too far. I will give you time. I won't come after you; I will wait for you to come to me when you are ready." Smiling Pike forced himself to look away., "Let's just not wait another thirty years..." His voice trailed off.

Maggie smiled and hugged him.

"No, not thirty years." She patted his cheek gently.

Maggie bundled up in an old Bolton College sweatshirt, paint stains splattered across the front. She strolled with her head down, trying to block some of the fine sand stinging her eyes. Finally giving up with wind and sand attacking her, she walked back to the protection of her cottage.

A few days after the conversation with Pike, Maggie sat in front of her easel on the porch. A canvas stared back at her. The conversation with Pike earlier in the week kept flashing back. She kept thinking of the secret that she held. She separated from Pike at the coffee table partly because she could not tell him about Tasha.

A white sheet of paper suspended on her easel on her front porch captured her attention. She picked up the easel and her paints placed them inside as the rain which had been threatening all morning arrived vigorously. She raced around the cottage closing windows. Finally, she stopped in the middle of the kitchen and sat down, breathing a loud sigh of relief. The rain pelted the roof and the bits of sand bit at the windows. Maggie felt like the storm attacking the cottage was like the storm that raged in full fury within her.

Grabbing her paint brushes, she lost herself in a flurry of color and imagination. An image appeared on the canvas resting on her easel. The storm subsided after a few hours as did the storm within her. Painting drained her of all the emotions rumbling around inside of her. She stood, grabbed a glass of water, and gulped it down. Sweat rolled down her face as she walked out the door to the porch. Sitting in her rocker, she rocked back and forth gently. Pike's image appeared in her mind. He morphed from the young college student to the man that she met again on Pelican Island. She saw him sitting at the table in the coffee shop and the way things ended. Maggie kept asking herself: What are you afraid of?

What if Pike never did cheat on you? She thought about the secret that she was still holding.

Maggie grabbed a windbreaker and headed back toward the beach. The sun had given up and clouds sailed across the sky. The sweet smell of rain made everything feel like new. She walked until she ended up in front of the coffee shop. Looking through the windows, she saw Pike sitting by himself writing in his journal. Maggie turned and walked back toward her cottage.

As she went, she realized that the time was coming when she would have to tell Pike about Tasha. Pike might just turn around and walk away. She thought about meeting Pike again after thirty years only to lose him again. She realized her hands were clenched and aching. She opened and closed her fingers, took a deep breath, and slowly exhaled. She slowed down her pace and began to walk slowly along the oceanfront. She was not surprised; she ended up at the jetty just beyond her house.

The walk along the beach in early morning did not have its usual electric feeling. Looking up, through overflowing eyes, she realized the white picket fence, half buried in the sand, marked the end of her journey and the safety of a home.

Closing the door behind her she slid into the old worn, brown leather lazy boy recliner. Her tears stopped, breathing slowed down, eyes grew tired, and closed.

Her mind replayed the scene in the coffee shop. She knew he was in as much pain as she was. Sometimes, love just hurts.

25

The regulars gathered in front of Maggie's cottage for their morning walk, but she did not appear. John knocked on her screen door, no answer. Turning back to the group he walked down the steps and onto the sand. The group turned away from Maggie's cottage and walked in the sand toward the edge of the sea. Even the dogs seemed quiet. Without a word, even from Rachel, they turned and followed their dogs down the beach.

As the group walked, Sandy thought about the conversation she had a few days ago with Maggie. Sandy and Maggie talked about men in their lives and found a common experience. Maggie talked about being a single mom. Sandy related her own story of being a single mom.

"I never expected to be one," Maggie said as she curled her toes in the warm wet sand.

"I was a single mom; my husband the father of our baby left us while we were still in the hospital," Sandy said.

Maggie thought about sharing her story with Sandy, then decided to share only part of it.

"My college boyfriend left after college; I did not see him again until several weeks ago."

Sandy and Maggie walked along the beach, holding onto some of their memories. Each was glad to know someone who understood what it was like to be a single mom.

"Most people don't understand how difficult it is to work and be a single mom at the same time. There were times when I did not know if I could handle it anymore." Sandy's voice trailed off.

Maggie turned to her. "Maybe being alone is the hardest part, not having someone to share the burden."

Sandy stopped walking, "I met my husband, Jack, when my daughter was fourteen years old. He is quiet, and probably not the easiest person to understand, but he loves me and my daughter."

Maggie's voice was tight. "My daughter is just turning thirty this year. I have not seen her for a few years. Sandy, thanks for the conversation. "I think I'm going to head on home." I feel like doing some painting and the light is perfect."

"Come on, you two," John's voice broke the moment between Sandy and Maggie. Sandy had picked up her pace and rejoined the group.

Rachel strolled up next to John as they walked. She leaned in toward him. John tensed as she stopped walking and put her hands on her hips, waiting for John to stop walking. The group walked on, following the dogs.

John stopped a few steps in front of Rachel; everything inside of him told him to keep walking. Her hands on her hips did not work. She crossed her arms across her chest.

"John, I know you can hear me," she whispered. The group was twenty feet down the beach.

John stepped back to Rachel. He stood in front of her, waiting for her to say something.

"John, what are you going to do? You know each of them better than anyone; it's your fault anyway," her voice took on an edge of authority. John was startled by her ability to focus everything on him whenever the group needed something.

"Me! How can it be my fault?" As soon as the words escaped his mouth, he knew that he'd opened an opportunity for Rachel to jump in.

The group, as if prompted by some outside director, murmured their agreement but kept their eyes glued to the sand at their feet. John shrugged his shoulders, hoping someone would say something or come to his rescue. No one did.

Rachel stared, her eyes digging into his being.

John looked around at the group, who gathered around the pair. John took a chance, "I will think about it if Rachel helps me."

The words caught the group and Rachel off balance. For as long as anyone remembered, Rachel was never speechless. There was a slight nod of her head and that was all John needed.

As the group walked down the beach, the conversation returned to the normal chit chat about the events of the past evening and the plans for the rest of the day.

In the last days of August, the island visitors packed up their beach chairs and ice chests and gathered sun burned kids for journeys back home. summer time romances end with promises to stay in touch. Their parents hoped they would not.

Uninhabited cottages and condos suddenly made Pelican Island silent, almost motionless.

The sun was a little less intense, the regulars wore long sleeved T-shirts in the mornings. Rachel did not stop at her home but continued with John as the last of the group disappeared. Arriving at John's cottage, they sat on the porch steps. Neither said anything for a while; then John broke the silence.

"Would you like some iced tea?"

She nodded, then several minutes passed before Rachel spoke. For a while they talked about Pike and Maggie as they sipped the cool tea in the waning hours of the morning.

"John, can you talk again with Pike? You've spent some time together." Rachel's voice was soft.

John looked puzzled as Rachel continued to talk.

"John, are you listening to me?"

"Rachel, what do you expect me to do? It is really none of our business."

"John, if you talk with Pike I will talk with Maggie."

"Rachel, really it's not up to us. I do not feel comfortable talking to Pike about this."

"Just give it a try. I will try to talk with Maggie. We haven't been on the best of terms, you know."

"They've spent a lot of time walking together on the beach at sunset and sitting in cafes," John said. "A few days ago, I saw them talking and it looked intense."

During the past months, Maggie and Pike roamed the beach together, oblivious to anyone else on the beach. Sometimes they walked with the group. However, more often, they walked alone or sat on the driftwood log and watched the pelicans glide across the surface of the sea.

The group decided John would talk with Pike. Before Rachel spoke, he knew this was going to be their plan. Looking around he saw Buddy come around the corner of the house. He sat in front of Rachel and John, taking turns looking at each of them. John knew Buddy needed water; he pushed the water dish in front of John.

"Very subtle, Buddy," John said as he picked up the dish and went into the house. Bud nudged Rachel's elbow. She moved over and gave him some space to sit between the two of them.

Rachel looked at Bud, "Subtle."

John came back with a pan of water for Bud and put it in the shade around the side of the house. Rachel smiled as she thought "subtle."

As far as Rachel was concerned, she'd settled the matter. She left it in John's lap. As she was getting ready to leave, he stood up and brushed sand from the back of his shorts. Seeing Rachel was fixing to get up, John reached out, took her hand, and helped her to her feet. Rachel noticed.

Later each would say something changed at that moment. The touch of the other's hands broke through a wall. Each at once pulled back their hands, causing Rachel to momentarily lose her balance. She sat down with an unlady like thump. Embarrassed, she quickly rose to her feet and started walking home.

John sat down on the step as Buddy walked over from the side of the cottage, his body wagging back and forth. Looking at Buddy, John whispered,
"What do you know that I don't know?"
Buddy came up, plopped down next to him, and, after one deep breath, fell asleep at once. John sat with Buddy's head in his lap and watched the endless waves dance across the light brown sand.

The sun moved above the horizon as seagulls conversed from the roof of his house. Stretching his arms over his head, one leg reached down to find his sandals. John threw back the covers and stepped into the middle of the room. The smell of coffee crept into his bedroom and beckoned him toward the kitchen. After slipping on a pair of worn blue jean shorts and a faded T-shirt from another day, he made his way to the kitchen. He slipped on a pair of worn blue jean shorts and a faded T-shirt.
Holding his mug in his hands, he walked out to the porch and heard the sounds of the waves crashing upon the shore. With a strong sea breeze, the waves grew more aggressive.

He called Rachel the night before to let her know he would not be walking with the regulars in the morning; he'd be heading to the coffee shop early to catch up with Pike. The second reason John wanted to hit the shop early was to grab a fresh maple Danish. In an agreement with himself, he had settled on one a week. Usually, it was Sunday morning. However, this would be his Danish day.
John had not thought about what he would say to Pike nor if Pike would even talk with him. Pike was a very private man and kept his feelings and his thoughts to himself. He and Pike had spoken

sometimes while sharing space on the driftwood log in the early mornings. Pike had not shared much, but did talk about his writing and the fact that he had come to the beach to find something he had lost. Grabbing two hot drinks and two Danish, John sat outside at a small picnic table under a faded blue umbrella. People walked by and greeted each other as they made their way into the shop. The smell of coffee brewing, and fresh baked breads and pies filled the air.

John pulled out a well-worn copy of The North Runner a book by DH Lawrence. Having read it so many times, he noticed some of the pages were falling out. A yellowed rubber band held the book together. With special reverence, John opened the book and began to read while waiting for Pike.

Pike appeared about fifteen minutes later. Pike looked up and his face flashed recognition. He also saw the two mugs of coffee and two Danish sitting on the table. John stood and beckoned Pike, pointing to two mugs and lure of warm pastry. With a slight smile, Pike walked over, shook hands with John, and sat down. Pike's face changed from recognition to suspicion.

"Why are you here and not with the others?" said Pike with an edge in his voice.

Talk started hesitantly between the two as if each was sizing up the other, wondering what the other wanted. It was John who broke through the verbal impasse.

"Pike, I have not seen you or Maggie for a few days. I was wondering if everything is ok?"

Words came out a little too fast, indicating John was nervous. Pike, having been a writer and an observer, did not miss the anxiety in John's voice.

Pike picked up his mug, took a sip, and looked straight into John's eyes. They were warm and welcoming. Pike put his cup down on the table.

"Maggie and I have decided to not see each other for a while. It was a mutual decision and is better this way."

Pike's words did not match his eyes or his lack of energy. John knew from his own experience, it was not time to push Pike, just to listen. The silence between the two lasted a while, as they both sampled the Danish and sipped their coffee. Sometimes silence is more powerful than a mouthful of words.

John reflected on a time when he had lost someone awfully close to him and, knowing his feelings then, he understood Pike's message though his words were few and silence encompassed both.

When sufficient time had elapsed, John asked Pike if he wanted to take a walk? Pike thanked John for the offer but said he would take a rain check. Pike was the first to stand. He turned, grabbed his backpack, and headed toward the beach. Pike turned around, looked at John, smiled faintly and said, "Thanks for the Danish and coffee." Then he was gone.

John finished his coffee and looked around for an excuse to stay. Finding none, he swallowed the last of his coffee and walked home.

Rachel was sitting on the steps to his porch by the time he reached home. John's stomach tightened as he walked the last fifty yards. Much to John's surprise, she did not ask him questions. She just sat watching a couple of porpoises playing in the surf.

The next morning the sky was blocked by low hanging dark clouds. The waves, backed up by the wind, attacked the beach more aggressively as the day progressed. Rachel said that the regulars had walked by his house; she'd decided to wait for him. John smiled for the first time that morning. He knew Rachel was fighting the urge to ask questions about his meeting with Pike.

John sat down next to her. The silence between them was comfortable. After some time, Rachel stood up, smiled at John, and thanked him for agreeing to meet with Pike.

"John, I know that was difficult for you to do this morning. I think it meant a lot to Pike." Her words were soft and comforting.

Pike walked alone through the town letting his legs carry him where they wanted. The breeze stiffened as it brushed his face. The temperament of mother nature reminded him of Maggie. Sometimes she was so soft and warm; other times she could be cold and argumentative. Pike stopped walking and let his heart recapture the warm times. He felt Maggie's hair when it lightly touched his face, coupled with her contagious giggle. Some images were difficult to forget.

A few days later, John stepped on the deck in front of the bakery. This time Pike sat with two cups of coffee and two maple Danish sweet rolls. Without a word, John joined Pike. Pike pushed a mug and a Danish across the table to John. John noticed the coffee was not as hot as usual. John wondered how long Pike had been waiting.

Pike sat with his back against the chair and started to talk.

His words came hesitantly at first. "I knew Maggie a long time ago; we met in college. When college ended, we went our separate ways, like in many college romances."

John leaned forward, his elbows resting on the table. "I met my wife in college also. I thought we would last forever. She died ten years after college. Then I moved here to Pelican Island." John leaned back in his chair.

The two men sat in silence for a while letting each other's words sink in. John decided not to share the information about Pike with Rachel for now.

John thought about Maggie and the pain that she seemed to be in when she arrived on the island. He knew there was more to the story.

"So, what are you going to do about it?" John's words were spoken with strength. He leaned into the table again catching Pike's attention.

Pike sat back in his chair, looking off toward the ocean. John's question was the same question he had been asking himself for the last two weeks. As he sat there looking at John, Pike thought about the last time he saw Maggie in college.

Pike looked at his hands resting on the table. He remembered driving up to Maggie's parent's house, he remembered being so scared. He rang the doorbell and Maggie's little sister came to the door.

"What do you want?" she shouted, then she shut the door. Pike stood on the small stoop in front of the house, not sure what to do. He turned around and started walking to his car, then stopped, turned around and walked up to the door again. Maggie's little sister was looking out her bedroom window. She ran to the door as Pike reached out to ring the doorbell again.

"She doesn't want to see you."

Maggie came to the door and pushed her little sister away from the door.

"What do you want, Pike? I told you I did not want to see you again."

"Maggie, what did I do?"

"Pike I trusted you with my heart. You broke it." Maggie's words just seemed to hang in the air.

"Maggie, but I..." Pike's words were cut off as the front door slammed shut.

The door opened again, and Maggie's father stepped out onto the stoop.

"I don't know what happened between you and my daughter. I trusted you with her. Get out of my yard; don't ever show yourself around my daughter or my house. You got five minutes to get into your car and get out of here or you and I are going to have a more serious conversation, and you will not like it. Now get out of here, before I kick your ass."

The words came slowly at first as a trickle burgeoning into a torrent as emotion took over.

The story that Pike told was how he and Maggie had met in college for the perfect match. The story ended with Pike telling how they were broken and lost touch with each other after graduation. The story was told with sadness and great puzzlement.

26

Maggie slowly opened her eyes and looked over at the clock on the nightstand. Blinking and squinting, she stared at its numbers, 5:00 a.m. It had been a long night of tossing and turning as she tried to understand something. With her eyes open, her mind slowly extracted thoughts from the sleepless night, trying to make sense of whatever it was she had tried to resolve.

Stretching her arms over her head, pushing a rebellious strand of hair from her face, she swung her legs first one, then the other to the floor. The coolness of the hardwood felt good on her feet. Standing, looking out the window, she realized the sun was up at this time of day. The thought of fresh coffee, beckoned her along with the thought of a hot shower. Coffee won. She pulled a faded T-shirt over her head and moved toward the kitchen. Grabbing a mug of coffee, she went back to her bedroom and pulled on a pair of shorts.

Heading to the front-screened porch, she settled into a black rocker, she bought at a flea market a few weeks ago. She put her feet up on the railing in front of her, sat back, and watched the sun rising over the eastern horizon. The sky turned red-yellow as the rays of the sun pushed back a black velvet curtain.

Pushing her hair back behind her ears, she put on a large flower-printed hat. The screen door slammed shut. She stepped into the cool sand.

She headed toward the sound of the waves. The beach was deserted this time of the morning. Sometimes having the beach to oneself was the best time of day.

Close to her house, the four-foot wall of stone jutted out into the ocean from the beach. She went there out of habit. With no one on the beach, she sat and listened to the waves and let her thoughts run wild.

A few evenings earlier, Rachel was surprised to see John, because he was not alone; Maggie was with him. There was something slightly unsettling about the image, making her catch her breath for a moment. She and John had known each other for years and talked but never anything else. Having always been the star of the regulars, she never had competition for his attention. Now there was someone else. Some of the regulars were beginning to pay more attention to this newcomer, Maggie.

Trying to calm herself, Rachel thought about Maggie and the stranger, Pike, who had appeared out of nowhere, now the major topic of conversation when Maggie was not walking with the group.

Looking up as she neared the rock wall, her private place, she saw someone else had invaded her space. Stopping, she squinted her eyes to see more clearly. It was someone painting on an easel. She realized it was Maggie, of course. Too late to retreat, Rachel acknowledged Maggie, waving at her. As Rachel continued walking toward Maggie, she saw that the painting cast a mood expertly. Stepping up behind Maggie after a cursory greeting, Rachel studied the half-finished painting in front of her.

Maggie's talent came through in the strength of the images she captured on canvas. With a quick intake of breath Rachel whispered "Beautiful." Maggie stepped back from her easel and dug her feet into the sand. The two women studied the painting. It captured everything beautiful about sunrise on a far horizon.

Neither knowing what to say, they just stared. Maggie broke the silence.

"Thank you." Her words came out a little tighter than she expected. Without a word, they both turned toward the rocks and found a place to sit. Staring at the sun creeping up the horizon, they found comfort in the silence.

Sometimes circumstances allow two people to talk and share what in other times might not have seemed appropriate. While sitting with their backs against the rock wall, they watched the sky change from an orange-red sunrise to a majestic blue, and a tenuous bond formed.

Not looking at each other, Rachel and Maggie talked about life, shared experiences. A mutual comfort somehow pulled them together.

Little did they know, each was dealing with feelings, and questions that were comparable. It would take some time before they would be able to share that part of their lives. For today, it was enough just to be able to sit, talk, and enjoy the beginning of a new day, and a new friendship.

27

As Rachel meandered along the beach, so many things were whirling around in her head. The conversation with Maggie was not what she'd expected. A deep sadness, just beneath the surface, hid behind Maggie's smile. The fact that Maggie did not mention Pike, after they'd spent a bit of time together, suggested a problem. One of Rachel's strengths was her ability to read people and get them to tell their stories.

Rachel had felt something the last few days trying to get her attention. As she neared John's house, she could see him sitting on his porch steps waiting for the regulars to stop by for their usual morning trek along the beach. She had only a few minutes to talk to John alone, without the regulars asking a lot of questions she did not want to answer.

John looked up, smiled as he spotted her approaching. The two old friends looked at each other and understood. Each working through something, not ready to explain in entirety.

"Good morning, John, what's up?" He got up from the steps, brushing sand from his shorts. "Good morning."

Rachel opened the screen door and stepped inside. John went into the kitchen and returned with a large pail of water for the dogs that would soon be waiting outside.

"John, I need to talk to you; can you stick around after the others leave?"

"Sure," John said cautiously.

The regulars walked toward them, taking their time. Some walked in the cool ocean waters, carrying their shoes or sandals.

The dogs ran and played in the surf. Seeing John, they made a dash to him. They knew there was always a treat in his pockets. The pack surrounded him, tails wagged, each pushing for his attention.

The group pushed the dogs out of the way, and formed a circle, around John and Rachel. Sandy watched John and Rachel closely. Something was different between them. What were they hiding? With the group now complete, they followed their dogs down the beach, all alert for treasures left by the tides. Gray clouds hurried across the sky.

Conversation seemed stilted as Rachel and John walked. Each sensed a change, but they were not willing to broach the subject. John purposely began drifting as far from Rachel as possible, while still remaining in the group. He walked up to Jason, the only other male member of the group.

They often talked about the news of the day. Jason, a retired stock market broker, had strong opinions about everything.

Each man knew there was a line not to cross in their world news discussions in the morning. John was happy just to have another male to talk to, especially this morning. Rachel had a sixth sense, an ability to get into his mind, whether he wanted her there or not. This was one morning he did not want to give her an opportunity.

From the corner of his eye, he peeked at Rachel. She walked with Sandy, and seemed deep in conversation. They spoke in low tones. Then, it happened. As John stole another glance at Rachel, she caught his eye and smiled. That smile said, 'I know you are hiding.' John quickly shifted his glance to the incoming tide. It was too late; John knew Rachel had seen him. It was only a matter of time until she would trap him and know everything.

Soon the regulars headed back to their homes. Buddy fell into pace with John. Reaching down, John rubbed Buddy's head. If dogs could smile, Buddy would have been grinning.

Sandy was the last of the regulars to leave the group and head off to her house.

John and Rachel fell into step with each other, neither of them making eye contact or speaking. Buddy, in turn, fell into step with him. "John," For some reason Rachel's voice startled him, "would you like to stop at my place for something to munch on?" An innocent question; however, John knew there was nothing innocent about it. She was looking for information and she knew John was hiding something.

He sat in white wicker rocker on the porch, with his feet resting on a railing.

Rachel came out from the house with a plate of fresh baked muffins. She sat down in her white wicker rocker and gently rocked back and forth. John took a muffin, figuring if he was eating he could not answer questions. Wrong. She turned in her rocker, "So, John, what is going on? You were awfully quiet this morning during our walk."

John twisted slightly and, stuffing another piece of muffin into his mouth, grasped for one more moment to organize his words before he spoke.

"I was just thinking..." As soon as the words were out of his mouth, he knew that he had played into her hand. It was like being in a room with only one door out, and she was standing in front of it. Swallowing hard, he turned to her and began to speak.

"Rachel, Maggie and the man sitting on the driftwood log were once in a relationship during college. They used to come to Pelican Island for college breaks. Pike and Tony were roommates. Tony called me a few months ago, letting me know that Pike would be spending the summer in his house during Tony's round-the-world trip with Julie.

"Then I got a call from Maggie wanting to reserve my rental

property. She'd heard about its availability from Tony. Tony and I decided we would do something to try and get them back together."

Rachel stood up and walked to the far end of the porch, staring out at the dunes in the distance.

"John," her voice was soft. He leaned forward to hear her words.

"I ran into Maggie this morning at the jetty. She was painting. She is an incredible artist. We had a long talk. I know she still really cares about Pike."

Rachel turned her rocker toward John, with a series of short jerking movements.

"What are we going to do about it?" There it was, the inevitable question John had been expecting and dreading ever since he saw her sitting on his porch steps this morning. He knew, for better or worse, she had the next part of the plan worked out in her mind.

"John, you are going to have to talk with Pike," Rachel said.

"About what?" He rolled his eyes. Even as he spoke, he knew it was a weak counter move.

Rachel did not reveal what she knew. She would at the right time, and this was not it. John reluctantly agreed to think about their conversation, as if he could think of anything else during the rest of the day. As he walked home, he resolved to meet with Pike again, but not to share with Rachel their conversation.

John was about to take the first step up to his porch when it hit him. He was concealing information from her, but she was also hiding something. Rachel had not given him any additional information. She should be a private eye and heaven help the poor suspect.

28

John awoke early the next morning. He sat on the edge of his bed thinking about the conversation with Rachel the night before. As he thought about it, he realized he was never in control of it. Rachel was always a few steps ahead of him.

John thought about other conversations in the past with Rachel. Something tickled his brain,

"Maybe it's okay that she led the conversation." John's words hit the walls of his bedroom and echoed back at him. John smiled; she really challenged him.

Even though it was early, John called Pike. He knew Pike would be up; he was like John, an early riser.

"Yeah, John, what's up?" Pike said, rubbing the sleep from his eyes.

"How about Do Drop In Coffee Shop in about an hour?"

"Sure, John, you buying?" Pike laughed and hung up. Pike decided he wanted to see what John really wanted. A quick shower and a pair of shorts, a T-shirt, and sandals, and he walked out the door.

There was a breeze off the water and bits of sand filled the air. The sun was hiding behind some gray cloud. Pike was suspicious.

John sat a table by the front window of the shop. He was sitting behind a large iced tea and a plate with an assortment of morning pastries. His glass was mid-way to his mouth when Pike walked through the doorway. Knowing Pike, John slid a large mug across the table to the empty chair.

John had been thinking about the conversation he was to have with Pike, but he still wasn't sure what he was going to say.

Pike sat down, reached for the coffee, and took a long sip glancing at John.

"Well, John, what's up?"

John took a sip of his tea. I have a project I need help with. I'm the president of the Pelican Island Historical Society. We're researching the history of the island. I'm good with my hands but not good at writing. I was wondering if you could help me research and write the journal. I'll buy dinner at the Lobster Shack and tell you more. John waited for the request to sink in.

"John, what is this really about?" said Pike as he took another sip of his lukewarm coffee.

John sat back in his chair- I really do have to write the history. I know you're a history major and a writer; I thought it was something you might be interested in.

Pike broke off a piece of his cinnamon pastry and pushed it into his mouth.

"Tony's cottage looks good with the new coat of paint. Is it holding up ok?"

"Ok, nice maneuver shifting to the paint, John. I guess I don't have a choice." Pike was grinning. "When do we start?"

"How about next week, today is Friday- would that work for you?"

John and Pike finished their pastry and walked out the door together. They agreed to meet on Monday for coffee and then go to the Pelican Island Library to start researching the project.

John walked back to his house, switching back and forth between smiling and feeling guilty. The smile won out. John tapped the top of his porch railing as he walked onto the porch.

He sat down in the rocker in his living room and called Rachel.

"Hi Rachel, do you by any chance still have the history of Pelican Island that you and I wrote years ago?"

Rachel thought about the project they worked on and the journal that they completed. "Yes, I think I still have a copy, why?"

"Oh, I'm thinking of updating it." John hoped she would remember all the arguments they had when writing the history.

"How much is it worth to you, John?" Rachel's voice had a cockiness to it. John knew she had him trapped.

I will make clam chowder and a blueberry pie," John said, hoping she would not ask a lot of questions.

"Ok, I'll bring wine. See you tonight around seven." Rachel sat back, wondering what he was up to. She felt confident she would be able to get John to let it slip.

After dinner that evening, Rachel flipped off her sandals and sat cross-legged on the couch. She picked up a pile of papers and began to read them.

"John, I don't remember all this research when we put together the journal," Rachel said as she yawned.

"Do you really think we need all this information? John, are you listening to me?"

"I was just closing my eyes, picturing how the journal will look when it's finished."

"How long have we been talking about this?"

John poured another glass of wine for Rachel and then filled his own glass.

"Let's put it aside for now," John said.

"There's an old movie on TV tonight. It Happened Last Night with Gable and Colbert."

Rachel and John sat on the floor with their backs up against the couch. During the movie, Rachel got up, put her head against the back of the couch, and fell asleep. John dozed off too and woke an hour later. He put a blanket over Rachel, went into his bedroom and again fell asleep.

29

The sun rose too early. As John tossed and turned in his sleep, it crept into his bedroom uninvited, spreading across his bed, poking, and prodding him from his sleep. As he opened his eyes, thoughts of Rachel came into focus. The conversation from the night before replayed. The two of them realized something was just beneath the surface but neither wanted to admit it.

Maggie and Pike in their lives had finally dislodged them from their complacency. It was the alliance of their effort to help their friends struggling in a relationship that made them look at themselves. Maybe it was the late night. Maybe it was the conversation with a few glasses of wine in the background as they talked into the early hours of the morning.

As John unscrambled his brain and made his way to the bathroom to take a quick shower, he heard his coffee maker gurgling in the kitchen. Faint footsteps of someone walking across the living room floor.

The door hinges to his room creaked and a splinter of light from the living room crept into his room. Rachel stood there still dressed in her wrinkled shorts and baggy sweatshirt from the night before. It was all coming back to him now. She had fallen asleep as they watched the movie on the couch. He'd put a pillow under her head and covered her with a blanket before crawling into his own bed.

She stood in the doorway with his mug in one hand and a plate of eggs and bacon in the other. Her hair still matted from sleeping. A smile existed just at the corners of her mouth and her eyes were still only half open.

"Good morning, sorry I fell asleep in the middle of the movie last night." Her words were muffled and still a little slurred from sleep or a little too much wine.

John reached out and took the cup and the plate. He'd tried brushing his hair back, seeking to make himself a little more presentable.

"Thanks," he said, his voice still raspy from sleep. He led Rachel out of his bedroom to the dining room and began to eat.

They sat in silence, not making eye contact. Each understood something was different between them.

John was the first to break the silence.

"You fell asleep so soundly," said John, "I just didn't want to wake you."

Rachel, coming out of her trance, looked up and realized John was talking to her.

"John, I enjoyed our conversation last night, the wine was perfect. I don't recall the movie. Remember, John, you will continue to talk with Pike and I will talk with Maggie."

Getting up from the couch, John stood and walked Rachel to the door and out onto the sand. The sun was beginning its journey from the horizon into the open sky. Rachel turned and started walking toward her house. She stopped, turned back toward John.

"Thanks for a great night," she said softly, as if the seagulls perched on the roof of John's cottage might hear her. She smiled, winked and was gone.

John stood for a long time wondering what was happening? He and Rachel had known each other for a long time and had clashed over conversations about politics, religion, friendships, and about everything two people could talk about. The energy sometimes rising between them quieted the others in the group of regulars. Sometimes they just listened and wondered about them. There had been private conversations amongst the regulars. Speculation about John and Rachel, and even some about John and Maggie.

However, those speculations ended when Maggie pulled away from the group and spent more time with the loner, Pike. He walked with the regulars a few times. He was always there ahead of them sitting on the driftwood log writing or just sipping his coffee and watching the ocean as if he could see something endlessly fascinating out there.

Often after the regulars passed by, Pike would walk the beach toward Morgan's jetty. Walking out on the rocks, he searched the small puddles of sea water left after the tides withdrew. Sometimes in the small backwater puddles he watched crabs and other tiny sea creatures. After walking out on the jetty he found a place to sit and write in his notebook.

Once Maggie had started to spend time with him, he would sometimes wave to the regulars as they walked by. John was the only one to take time to sit and talk with him. John didn't say much about what he and Pike talked about.

This morning Rachel chose not to join the regulars on their daily walk. She took a shower and headed for Maggie's cottage. She stopped on the way and grabbed two coffees and two blueberry muffins.

As she got closer to Maggie's house, her mind raced deciding what she would say. She knocked on Maggie's screened porch door.

"Maggie, are you up?" Rachel said as she stood on the first step up to the porch.

From somewhere inside, the sound of movement. The screen door opened, revealing Maggie dressed in baggy yoga pants and a T-shirt. Her hair was a mass of tangled strands shooting out from her head as if struggling to escape. Rachel smiled as she thought about her own appearance some mornings. Maggie spied the coffee and bag from the coffee shop, opened the screen door, and let Rachel in.

The two women sat on the porch, rocking and sipping their

coffee. Rachel broke the silence, choosing her words carefully after spending time with Maggie on the beach a few days ago.

"Want to go to the rocks?" Rachel said, as if someone else was there to hear her.

"Sure, let me get my sandals, I'll join you on the beach." Why was Rachel here this early in the morning? What was on her mind?

30

Maggie and Rachel stepped into the sand from her porch and headed for Morgan's jetty, which stretched into the sea about a hundred yards away. Centuries of changing tides had smoothed the rocks.

The sun crawled above the far horizon, as Maggie finally felt her heart slow down and the rocks came into view.

The summer crowds had disappeared, as summer gave way to a brisk autumn. The wall of rock was always a place to sit and ponder the deeds of the day, or even the events of her life past and present.

Rachel's visit in the morning had been something unexpected. They had met once for coffee and shared glimpses of each other's lives as a way of testing the waters with each other. The meeting at the rocks last week was also unexpected but had turned out to be enjoyable for both.

Rachel had let down her guard a little, as they talked at the rock and this morning even more so. Maggie was slow to open up to others, especially women. She'd been burned in the past and now held back in her sharing.

Maggie kept to herself all things connected to her emotional life. But it was not always that way. Pike had helped her to try new things and always seemed so open during those early days.

Rachel sat with her back against the rocks watching Maggie. She had stopped talking and seemed to be in some other place.

"A quarter for your thoughts..." Rachel's words interrupted Maggie's thoughts. Looking up, she realized Rachel was staring at her, waiting.

"I'm sorry, what were you saying?" Maggie's words no more than a whisper.

"It seems like you were far away."

"Sometimes the moments at separate times in my life push their way into my present uninvited. I find myself thinking more and more about Pike. Men!" Maggie shook her head.

Rachel smiled as she raised her cup toward Maggie.

"My grandmother rephrased the old saying. She'd declare, "Men: can't tolerate them and ya can't leave them alone!

Maggie and Rachel smiled. Both knew exactly what was meant.

An extra cool breeze swept in off the waters of the Atlantic. Sometimes more was expressed with a few words than a whole mouthful. Rachel got up and took another look at Maggie's painting.

"Your painting captures the rocks and the ocean--their endless battle just like the love/hate relationship between men and women."

Walking down the beach toward her house, Rachel felt she had found someone with whom she could let her guard down. She thought about the similarities between she and Maggie. Each kept a tight rein on their past.

31

As Maggie reached the rocks, the waning rays of the sun settled just above the horizon, creating shadows. Dusk settled around the rocks. The heat from the day was still in the warmth of the rocks on her back. She settled into the sand and sat back against the wall. Pulling her knees up toward her chin, she looked down the deserted beach. The last of the summer folks had retreated from the island weeks ago.

She had not seen Pike since the day in the bakery, but she had not stopped thinking about him. His image crept into her mind at odd times during each day. As she closed her eyes she could see him sitting across from her in the coffee shop. Words had flown from her mouth during that last encounter.

They came from somewhere deep inside. The pain of seeing him again after all these years and sharing time together seemed too easy. Setting aside the hurt, it was as if they had never separated.

Memories of him walking away after college pierced her but she wondered if what he'd wanted to say really would have changed anything.

She was not sure how many of her memories were accurate, or had the passage of time rearranged some of them?

One memory was clear in her mind, the moment when she realized that it was over with Pike. He cheated on her with some freshman girl.

In the weeks following graduation, she started a job as a teacher and found an attic apartment. The old lady that owned the house invited her down for supper and became a good friend. Around the end of September, she realized she was pregnant with Pike's baby. Pike was gone; she had no idea where he lived.

She rested against the rock wall and thought about the first few months after she discovered she was pregnant. The phone call to her mother was the most difficult.

She sat on the floor in her apartment with her hand on the phone. Slowly she dialed her home phone, hoping her father wouldn't answer. The phone rang forever.

"Mom, its Maggie, can we have lunch tomorrow at the Villa Restaurant?"

"What's wrong?" Maggie's mother held her breath waiting for Maggie to say something.

"On second thought, Mom, I'll meet you at home around noon."

Maggie put the phone back on the receiver and let the tears fall. There was a knocking at the door. Maggie sat quietly, hoping that whoever was at the door would go away.

"Maggie, are you alright?" Mrs. Sansone asked.

"Yes, Mrs. Sansone, I'm ok."

"I made some chicken soup and was wondering if you would like some."

She opened the door and accepted the soup from her landlady.

"Thank you so much." Maggie placed the soup on the table and hugged her.

"Things always look darker at night. Good night, dear."

The next morning Maggie drove by her parent's house a bit early, and her mother's car was sitting in the driveway. Maggie pulled into the driveway. Mother walked out through the back door and hugged her daughter. With an arm around Maggie's shoulders, she walked with her into the house. The house was empty but felt warm and inviting.

Grandmother's bone china teapot sat on the kitchen table. Two matching tea cups and saucers sat in front of a Wedgewood plate of chocolate cookies.

Maggie looked at the table and started to cry.

"Mom, I'm pregnant. I am pregnant with Pike's baby and I don't know where he is."

————)(()(————

The years of rebuilding her life and raising a baby were difficult. Her father never forgave Pike for getting his daughter pregnant and abandoning her. Maggie's father didn't know the story of Pike cheating on her.

He only knew that his daughter had a broken heart. However, if Pike was around at that time, he would have had to stay far away from her dad. The baby grew into a headstrong young woman. Tasha never knew her real father.

During Thanksgiving break from college her junior year, Tasha spent a week at home with her mother. Tasha had a ride from college with a couple of friends who lived in the same community. They planned to get together later for drinks and music at Telly's Pub, the only place nearby that had pizza and music.

Maggie went out grocery shopping, expecting Tasha later in the afternoon.

Tasha arrived earlier than expected. She rang the doorbell. No answer. She searched for the key to the front door, always hidden in one of the planted pots on the front stoop. Annoyed, she knew her mother moved the key so someone wouldn't break in and kill her daughter and herself. That is what her mother had told her ever since she was a little girl.

She found the key in a potted geranium plant that looked like it was on its last legs. Brushing the dirt off the key she opened the door.

"Mom, are you here?" Tasha walked into the kitchen and

opened the refrigerator. There was a note hanging from the milk carton.

"I have gone grocery shopping. There are homemade chocolate chip cookies in the cookie jar. Love you, Mom."

"Very funny, Mom." Tasha laughed. It was a standing joke that her mother always left a note for her in a place she thought her daughter would go first when she arrived.

She went into her mother's bedroom, searching for a sweater to wear later in the evening. She opened the closet doors, and pushed the hangers aside as she scanned the sweaters, turtlenecks, and pullovers all arranged by color.

A light blue sweater caught her eye. She pulled the hanger out for a closer look. The sweater dropped off the hanger and fell to the floor. Getting on her knees, she pushed the hanging dresses and blouses out of her way looking for the blue sweater. A bulging red shoebox peeked out from underneath a pile of shoe boxes.

The red box was wrapped with frayed gold ribbon. Tasha pulled the shoebox out from under the pile and sat down with the box on her lap. Delicately she pulled a strand gold ribbon, the strand broke in her fingers. Opening the box gently, Tasha saw a small red diary with her mother's initials in the bottom right corner. Tasha looked at a picture glued to the inside top of the box. Two couples stood in front of an old car. Everybody had their arms around each other. The picture looked like one continuous smile across the group.

The box was stuffed full of letters in envelopes. Another picture of a girl and a guy sitting next to a fire on a beach. She recognized her mother. The two were kissing.

Maggie grabbed a couple of bags from the back seat and walked to the front door. The sounds of music hit her as soon as she put the key into the lock. Tasha was home. With the opening of the front door, Tasha put the box back into the corner of the closet with some other boxes on top of it just like she'd found it. Grabbing her mother's blue sweater, she ran out of the room in time to see her mother come through the front doorway, hands wrestling with two large bags of groceries. Maggie called for help. It was no use. The music blocked her voice from reaching Tasha. Tasha came through the door into the kitchen in time to catch one of the bags falling out of her mother's hands.

"I've got it, Mom."

The sound of a dog and someone walking toward her pulled Tasha back to the present. Looking up, she saw a blond woman about sixty years old walking in her general direction with a full-sized poodle.

After sitting on the steps to the white cottage it felt good to stand up and stretch her back and arms. The trip from Chicago to Pelican Island had been a long trip. She was not even sure when she started the drive that she would end up at her mother's place. But, with no other place to go, her car just seemed to end up here on its own.

Meanwhile, the woman rapidly moved closer, only about a hundred feet from the steps of the cottage. She seemed to be talking to the dog as if the dog understood every word. The woman turned her attention to Tasha. "Are you looking for someone?" the voice was shrill and not very friendly.

"I'm looking for my mother. I think she's staying in this cottage." Tasha realized that she was giving information to a perfect stranger, and took a step back from the woman and her pure white poodle.

"Who is your mother?" Again, the woman's voice did not convey any warmth, just a feeling of interrogation.

Tasha explained who she was and the woman's taut demeanor evaporated instantly, but a puzzled look crept across her face. "My name is Rachel. I'm a friend of your mother's." A sudden smile slipped across her face. Gone was the shrill sound in her voice, replaced with a voice that oozed like honey.

"Your mother is probably down by the rocks. She sometimes goes there to paint."

As soon as Tasha gave up her name, the two of them started walking toward the rocks; Tasha wondered if she'd fallen into a spider's web. Who was this woman who could switch moods on a dime?

However, in the distance Tasha could see a lone figure sitting by the rocks looking out at the ocean. She seemed lost in her thoughts.

As quickly as she'd appeared, Rachel turned and started walking in the opposite direction. She had enough information to share with John.

Maggie looked up and saw her daughter. So many thoughts raced through her mind. She and Tasha had ended at an ugly place the last time they'd seen each other. Words seemed to spit out of each as they spoke. Tasha had stormed out of the condominium in Chicago. The door had slammed shut and neither of them had spoken in the four months that Maggie had been at the beach. As Maggie watched her daughter walk toward her, she noticed that her daughter was pregnant.

Both women walked toward each other, then stopped, each waiting for the other to make a move. Tears seemed to appear on each of their cheeks at the same time. Arms outstretched Maggie moved toward Tasha. But they fell back to her side when she saw the expression on Tasha's face

Tasha looked at her mother and noticed the sadness in her eyes and the loss of weight. Maggie looked at her daughter and did a mental evaluation, noticing the red eyes and her daughter's failure to make eye contact with her.

As mother and daughter walked toward Maggie's cottage, the empty space between each of them seemed like an uncrossable chasm. Maggie waited patiently to let her daughter talk. Maggie touched her daughter's shoulder gingerly. With that simple physical contact, the words and emotions began spilling out of Tasha. She broke and released all the fresh anger and emotion she'd been carrying around for the last few months. Maggie put her own feelings and thoughts of Pike away to be there for her daughter.

Tasha had broken up with her boyfriend. As the tears rolled down her daughter's cheeks, tears from Maggie's pain matched her daughter's. Maggie could not help feeling a strong dose of déjà vu.

Tasha stood as stiff and unmoving as a fence post as Maggie whispered in her daughter's ear, "I love you."

29

Maggie was heartbroken that her daughter was in the same place that she was when she and Pike split up after college. Maggie had been determined not to let her daughter end up the same way that she had.

Sometimes it takes a lifetime for a story to be told from beginning to end. Maggie and Tasha sat on the porch steps of the cottage watching the approaching storm. The sun slowly disappeared below the horizon. The air grew static with their silence, as each waited for the other to break the wall. The heart sometimes holds words hostage, wrapped tightly around the emotions of the heart.

There was a distant rumble of thunder and a lightning flash across the Atlantic. Both women looked up at the darkening sky. Again, the lightning flashed, and thunder exploded. Maggie and Tasha retreated to the shelter of the porch. Sitting on the porch rockers, Maggie rocked gently; Tasha rocked violently.

Maggie was the first to break the silence. The first few words struggled to escape her heart. Then like opening a floodgate, everything that Maggie had stored away came rushing out, surrounding her daughter and shutting out the world about them. The abruptness of her words caught Tasha by surprise.

"Your biological father was a guy I knew during my college days."

Maggie's words were spoken softly. Even more powerful were the words that Tasha spat back. "I know that, Mom, I've known for a long time." Tasha's words were charged with anger, finally released. Maggie reached out with her left hand to Tasha's hand. Tasha recoiled as if someone had pushed all the air out of her body.

"No Mom! It is not that easy; who is my father?" Her words pushed Maggie away. Maggie stopped rocking and watched her daughter. Maggie got up and walked into her house. She returned with a small red box.

"Tasha, I have something I want to share with you, if you're ready."

"Mom, I know about the red box in your closet. I found it when I was home from college during my junior year." More tears flowed.

Maggie leaned in toward her daughter and started the long story that was long overdue. All the while, Tasha crossed her arms across her chest, glaring. Then she turned and stared out at the approaching storm.

Another clap of thunder rolled across the sky.

Maggie looked at her daughter. "My story started a few years before your story started.

"I met a guy during the first week of college. There was a dance. We started talking and ended up together for the next four years. We'd planned to get married after college." Maggie's voice grew stronger as she told her story. "We broke up just before graduation. He left after graduation and I never heard from him again. A few months later I discovered that I was pregnant with you. I became a single mom at twenty-three years old.

"That part of my life was over, I never told you about him because I thought I would never see him again." Maggie stopped and looked at her daughter.

Tasha had turned to face her mother.

"That makes no sense. Don't you think I deserved knowing about my father? I always thought it was because of my faults that my father didn't want any part of me." The tears rolled down

Tasha's cheeks. She got up, walked out the door and headed toward the ocean.

Tasha, with anger still pulsating through her body, just followed the beach for a while. Off in the distance a driftwood log protruded from a sand dune almost covered in grasses waving in the breeze of the Atlantic. It was part of the trunk of a tree washed up on the beach years ago.

With tears of anger from somewhere deep inside, she collapsed on the log and lost herself as the sea gulls screamed at each other as they competed for food.

The words of her mother played on an endless loop in her mind. She thought back to the time when she found the battered box in her mother's closet and the love letters that were carefully tied with a gold ribbon. It did not make sense to her then; they were love letters from a boyfriend during her mother's college days. Why had she kept them all these years?

Over the years she'd wondered, who was this Pike who had sent her all these letters? She did not know if that was a first name or a last name. There was no mention of her mother being pregnant in any of the letters. There had been many times over the years she wanted to ask her mother about the letters.

After her discovery, when she went back to look again at them the box was gone. There was never another chance to explore the contents.

As Tasha sat and watched the gulls the anger welled up within her and seemed to have no ending. Thinking of her mother, a feeling of betrayal gnawed at her mind.

Maggie sat still in her rocker as her daughter walked away. Maggie felt she should let her have some space. As the rain eased to a misty drizzle, Maggie got up and walked to the rocks, her place of peace.

Maggie sat down, leaned back against the warm rocks, and thought about the day Tasha was born. It was a bitter freezing day in Chicago. There was a forecast for a February snowstorm.

She thought about the first time her baby kicked, she was with her mother talking about what it was like to have a baby.

"Mom, something just happened; it felt like the baby wants out immediately." Maggie rubbed her hands over her belly.

"It's all normal, Maggie," her mother said reassuringly.

Maggie sat in the doctor's office when her baby kicked again. It was not the first time. She put her hands on her belly. Oops, again a little kick.

She looked around the room. She was the only one sitting alone. Some couples were sharing baby-holding time with each other. Maggie knew she would be a single mom. So many emotions were flying around inside her. One moment she felt on top of the world and the next she was in tears.

"Maggie, you can see the doctor now." The nurse's voice was flat, like a Walmart greeter.

Maggie gathered her purse and used her arms to hoist herself off the chair. She waddled to the doctor's waiting room. The due date was just a week away. This was the last visit to the doctor's office before the due date.

Dr. Marion, a young woman in her mid-thirties, greeted Maggie as she stepped into the waiting room. An even younger woman trailed behind her.

"Maggie, do you mind if my intern sits in on this session?" said Dr. Marion Spencer, her voice full of excitement. "Well, we are getting close."

Maggie thought about what she said and looked at the doctor. "What do you mean we?"

"Oh, I am going to be with you the whole time. Nothing to worry about."

"Dr. Marion is a great doctor, she's been a doctor for three years," said the young intern, full of life and wonder.

Well, Dr. Marion was correct; the baby came right on time. The doctors and the interns were there with reassurance as they prepared Maggie for the birth of her baby. The ordeal of birth seemed to go on forever, but the casual banter of the doctor and nurses never changed. Finally, at 12:01 Saturday morning, Tasha was born. She entered the world with dark hair and bright blue eyes. She came into the world kicking and screaming.

The doctors wrapped Tasha in a blanket and handed her to Maggie. The baby lay upon Maggie's chest. The warmth of the baby and warmth of Maggie's skin seemed to finally soothe the newborn.

———— ◉ ————

Maggie sat with her back braced against the rocks of the jetty. She looked up. It was Tasha with a handful of chocolate chip cookies—her favorite as a child. She handed her mom cookies from one hand. They each began to consume the cookies slowly, as if meditating.

Slowly the words buried long ago the wall between mother and daughter began to collapse. Maggie looked at her daughter and saw herself in her daughter's eyes.

There were so many questions to ask so many things that she wanted to know about her real father. Over the next week many painful words flew back and forth between mother and daughter. As Tasha and Maggie thrashed around absorbed in their mother-daughter battle, life went on.

The regulars talked about the absence of Pike and the disappearance of Maggie during the past few weeks.

The group also noticed there was a difference between John and Rachel. There was a tension that was not there before or at least not the same kind of tension. Before it was a kind of two different personalities tension; now it was something else.

32

The shop's screen door had screeched as it slammed against its door frame. Pike watched Maggie, as she once again walked out of his life. He sat at a small table in the corner. A hush filled the room. The other patrons were witnesses to the argument between Pike and Maggie. Pike felt like all eyes were on him. But slowly the sounds of people talking and laughing replaced the silence.

Pike picked up his cup, swirled the grounds in the bottom of his mug, as his anger seethed just below the surface. Once again she had run out without letting him know what the problem was.

During those weeks that followed the break up, he just sat in his apartment, staring at his phone. The wound was fresh. Attempting to figure out what happened, he picked up his phone, started to dial her number, then put the receiver back into its cradle. Hanging up the phone meant that the conversation and relationship with Maggie was over.

He lay down on his old faded red couch, closed his eyes; images of so many times together during college flooded his mind. In a collage, images and words from his relationship with Maggie bombarded his heart. Finally, as the sun set, his eyes closed. Sleep was not an escape; conversations of his college days played in his mind.

Pike shook his head and glanced around the coffee shop; his coffee had grown cold, as had his heart. Grabbing his journal and pens and pencils, he ripped open his backpack and shoved them in. Throwing his backpack over his left shoulder, he marched out into the early evening. A cloak of darkness fits his mood.

"NOT AGAIN"!" he shouted as he walked along the water's edge. The words broke the silence around him, surprising him.

"NOT AGAIN!" his words repeated with more intensity. He turned around and headed toward Maggie's cottage. Whatever was bothering her, he was going to at least get the chance to let her know what he was feeling. The anger within him pushed him toward her cottage.

Standing outside on her porch, he hesitated. There were no lights on in the house. He knocked on the door--no response. He sat on the steps of the porch. The waves gently caressed the beach, the only sound.

Pike waited for a while, then remembered John had mentioned Maggie often went to the rocks just beyond her cottage to paint and think. He headed toward the rocks. In the moonlight, he saw a silhouette of someone. He walked closer.

"Maggie, it's me, Pike." at first there was no response. Moving closer, Pike could see that she was crying. Not waiting for an invitation, he sat down next to her.

Neither said anything for a long time, they just sat there staring out at the empty beach.

"Maggie, I want to know, what is going on between us? When we broke up after college, I never asked you why? I am not running away from you this time.

I love you and always have." Pike's words touched her. Silence once again filled in the spaces around them. The sounds of Maggie gently crying reached out to Pike. "Talk to me."

"You cheated on me." Maggie's knees pulled up tight under her chin, her arms wrapped around her legs, her words muffled.

Pike turned to look at her, Maggie, I've told you: I never cheated on you, I loved you."

"What about that freshman girl? She came to me and told me you were going to break up with me, the two of you had sex."

"Why did you believe her? Why did you never ask me about it? After everything we had been through, you never gave me a chance. You just believed her and not me.

"Maggie, as I told you, I did go to her dorm room. I had an article for the college journal she had to read for the next day. When I got there, she started kissing me. I pushed her away and told her that I was in love with you. She started taking her clothes off. I left.

"I ran into one of your friends coming out of her room across the hall from Nancy's room." I didn't know what to do. I walked to your dorm room to talk with you, but you had gone back to your parents for the weekend. That is the truth—swear to God. Yes, I should have told you. I just didn't know what to do. Tony and I spent half the night trying to figure out what I should do. I should have told you, but I was so afraid you would not believe me, and I would lose you.

"As it turned out, I did lose you." Pike's words came softly.

"Pike, why didn't you force me to listen to you? You just left. Why didn't you make me listen to you? I loved you.

You're right, the girl across the hall called me and told me you were in Nancy's room. And Nancy was so happy to tell me you were in her room. This Nancy came into the student union when I was having breakfast and made a big scene. She told me she had sex with you. Pike, my friends were there and heard everything. It was the ultimate humiliation."

The conversation continued as the night slipped away. The moon spread its light over the rocks and the glimmer of the ocean created a small secluded space for two people as they began to tear down walls and build some bridges.

Maggie guarded herself from releasing the one secret that she could not talk about. She could not open the closet of her memories about being pregnant when Pike left. She avoided his eyes, knowing that he was so good at reaching inside her heart.

Maggie and Pike stood up, each attempting to understand all the feelings that were running around in their heads.

Maggie's cottage appeared as they walked. Pike looked up at her cottage, stopped at the bottom of her porch steps. Each stood looking at each other. Pike reached out, put his arms on her shoulders. She reached up and put her hands on his arms.

"I am glad you came to find me." Maggie's voice was soft as she looked into his eyes. Once again thoughts of her daughter forced her to look away.

The next few days, Maggie and Pike stayed away from each other, each attempting to figure out what they were feeling and trying to make sense of the past and the present.

33

Grabbing his backpack and his journal, Pike headed for the Do Drop In coffee shop. The coolest weather of the fall season seemed to even discourage day tourists from Pelican Island. Summer does not last forever as a season, nor does it last forever as a season of our lives. The fall season of Pike's life had arrived, creating a need to settle some things left undone.

He looked around for his journal. The muse that had been avoiding him watched him from the corner of his mind. Softly at first, then a little stronger, the whispers of the muse began to make sense. Words clogged in his brain began to flow onto his journal.

The story had started strong and then dried up over the past few months. Now it was time to reawaken. Lost in his thoughts, his words raced across the pages of his journal. The characters' hidden story now began to take shape in his mind.

As he wrote, time slipped by without his notice. Pushing back his chair, he grabbed his cup and went inside for a refill. Pike realized hours had slipped away, the people in the coffee shop were different, gone was the frantic dash of the early morning caffeine addicts. Now people sat leisurely sipping their drinks and communicating in their own way.

Standing in line, he noticed a pretty young woman sitting by herself in a corner away from the other patrons. She was listening to something on her headphones, her foot tapping to some unknown rhythm as she slapped the keys on her computer. Watching, Pike noticed that her concentration never wavered even when she reached out and grabbed her cappuccino.

She must have reached the bottom of the cup, because she suddenly walked over and stood in line behind Pike. She smiled at Pike like someone delivering two messages: 'Hello' and 'Do not bother me' at the same time. Pike noticed her eyes first. They were a light blue, just like his.

"Work or pleasure?" Pike's words caught her by surprise as she escaped from her private world.

"I beg your pardon?" Her words seemed cold and annoyed as she kept her eyes on the mug in her hands. Suddenly uncomfortable, Pike repeated the question "Are you working on something for work or something for pleasure?"

Hoping to end the conversation, she told him that she was working on a short story for a writing contest. Without further delay, Pike introduced himself as a writer.

Realizing that the conversation was not going any further, Pike returned to his table with his coffee. Glancing at his watch, he realized that it was time to leave. Gathering his backpack and writing journal he headed for the door. After one last glance at the young writer, Pike slipped out the door and headed for the beach.

34

Pike rolled over in his bed, trying to block the sun from intruding into his room. The warm fingers of the sun searched his bed, blankets and pillows, seeking to expose him. As the sun crept higher into the sky, he surrendered. Slipping his legs over the side of the bed, he made his way to the bathroom. A cool shower finally woke him up.

An hour later, his eyes were wide awake and his mind was fortified with coffee and two muffins. Thoughts of what he was going to say to Maggie when he saw her kept him up most of the night tossing and turning.

It was time to try winning Maggie's heart and stop running away from her and all the other relationships in his life.

Stepping onto the porch, Pike took a deep breath. A soft rain filled the air with a freshness like a rebirth of something in his life.

For the first time since arriving on Pelican Island, he had been able to finish the short story sitting on his dining room table.

He grabbed his backpack and journal. With his trusty umbrella Pike stepped into the coffee shop to obtain a little more caffeine, before getting together with Maggie. He struggled to put his thoughts together into some coherent plan. The one thing he knew was that he was not going to run anymore. Standing up a little straighter, he put a spring in his step.

Pike slipped off his flip-flops and walked barefoot along the damp sand washed by the incoming waves. He stopped, looked down. A pure white sand dollar lay just out of reach of the incoming waves. It was perfect. He bent down and examined the treasure, turning it over.

It was the first time he had ever found a whole sand dollar. He took it as a good omen. He suddenly recalled a time when he and Maggie walked the beach during their junior year at college. It was the first time they'd gone away together. There was some tension between Maggie and Pike. They had been walking and talking about the beach and their relationship and expectations.

Pike figured they would sleep together; after all there were only two bedrooms. Maggie thought that Pike would sleep on the couch in the living room.

"Pike, I love you, but I am not ready yet to sleep together."

"Maggie, we've been talking about it. I love you." Pike and Maggie sat down on a driftwood log and shared their feelings about the future.

"Pike, I don't want to lose you. I am just not ready yet."

"Maggie, I'm not going anywhere without you. I'll sleep on the couch."

Pike smiled as he thought about that night. Maggie came into the living room in the middle of the night, took his hand and led him into the bedroom. Maggie wore shorts and a T-shirt; Pike wore his college T-shirt and pair of baggy shorts. They woke up in the morning wearing the same clothes. That was the night that things changed. Pike stopped pushing and Maggie stopped pulling away.

Pike put the sand dollar into his pocket and continued walking back toward the bakery. He remembered how much Maggie loved sand dollars. He stopped worrying about what he was going to say to her.

The coffee shop was busy as usual with the morning regulars. The same people seemed to come and go at the same times every day. As Pike stepped into the shop, he noticed the young woman sitting in a corner table now writing in a journal just like the ones that he wrote in every day.

Getting his coffee, he walked over to her table and she looked up and smiled faintly. There was something about her smile that made him catch his breath. Something familiar, something welcoming.

"Good morning, mind if I join you?" The words seemed tight as they tumbled out of his mouth. She looked up, closed her journal.

"No, I guess not," the words were so softly spoken that Pike had to lean in to catch the word.

Sitting down at the empty table next to hers, he put a splash of creamer into his coffee, opened his journal and began writing. After he had written a few pages in his journal, he noticed she was gazing at a blank sheet of white paper that stared back at her. Pike took a sip of coffee and put his pen down.

"What are you working on?" Pike said.

"Actually, I'm not working on anything. I am going around and around with a story I'm writing. I think my muse died!" She laughed. She broke off a piece of a blueberry muffin sitting on a paper plate in front of her.

"I thought my muse died a few months ago, but it has come back to life. Muses are tricky. Tell me your story," said Pike.

She sat there looking at the page in her journal. She flipped back a few pages and began to read

"No, don't read it; why not tell me the story?"

She closed her notebook, leaned back in her chair, sipped her coffee. Then put the cup back on the table.

"It is about two people who meet in college and end up breaking up at the end of four years."

Pike spit his coffee on the table. He turned away and wiped his mouth hoping she hadn't noticed.

She asked him about his work. He flipped back a few pages in his journal and started to read.

She looked at him mockingly, "Don't read it; tell me about it." She sat back and watched him reflect on his poem.

155

Pike laughed.

As they sat talking about writing and the frustration of finding just the right word, time slipped away.

With a start, Pike realized that all the energy that he had mustered for his meeting with Maggie was slipping away. The determination that had fired him up earlier in the morning evaporated during the last couple of hours. He left the shop and headed back to his house.

Looking down at the sand and the treasures the early morning tide had washed ashore, he did not notice Maggie walking toward him.

Maggie meandered along the beach, letting the waves wash over her feet. She noticed Pike walking in her direction. It seemed almost inevitable on this small island world that they would run into each other.

She had so many things to tell him, but was not sure how to do it. A few sleepless nights had robbed her of her energy.

Looking up from the sand, Pike stopped abruptly, spilling coffee on his T-shirt. Maggie stood about twenty feet away, watching. They both just stood there staring at each other, neither knowing what to do.

Pike looked down at his T-shirt.

"Come on, how can I spill my coffee twice in one day?" Pike looked at his T-shirt and burst out laughing.

Maggie put her hand to her mouth, trying not to laugh.

"Pike, I seem to remember you wearing your coffee well in college." Maggie burst out laughing.

As they laughed a couple of people walked by.

"Guess I'd better go everywhere lugging an extra shirt."

"I know the feeling," a man about Pike's age said and started to smile.

Maggie watched Pike and remembered his sense of humor. She'd forgotten about his ability to laugh at himself. She missed that.

It was the first time that they'd crossed paths since they last spoke at Do Drop In. All the thoughts that had run around in Maggie's mind now just seemed to disappear, leaving her with no clarity.

Pike took a long deep gulp of his remaining coffee, then moved toward Maggie. They felt like two thirteen-year olds facing each other in the school hallway, each trying to figure out what to say as their feet carried them closer to each other.

"Hey, why don't we…" as soon as the words were out of his mouth he wanted to reach out and pull them back. They seemed to just stick there in the space between them. Maggie looked up to Pike.

Not much more than a whisper from Maggie, "Yeah, hey, why don't we?" Their silence engulfed them, shutting out the rest of the world. Time stopped about five feet from each other. Finally, the silence became like a wall between them.

Pike said he had to get back to his place, turned and started walking away. What about all the self-talk he'd practiced? He was running away again. He stopped and faced Maggie.

Nothing on a small island goes unnoticed. Rachel watched Maggie and Pike from her porch.

Maggie's arms dropped to her sides. She looked up at Pike. Pike put both hands behind his head as he listened to Maggie.

"Pike, give me a little time to think about what is happening between us. Please don't leave me."

Pike reached out and took Maggie's hands in his.

"Maggie, I lost you once. I really don't want it to happen again."

Maggie put her arms around Pike and each held on as if afraid the other would disappear again.

"Would you like to get together again?"

"Yes," the word came from her quickly, and she waited for Pike to say when, but he just said 'Good.'

Each turned and started walking away. Each carried a small smile hidden from the other.

Rachel smiled. What made it especially sweet is that she knew something John did not. The only question in her mind was what she could do with this information. She smiled as she rocked back and forth in her wicker rocker.

36

After the encounter with Pike on the beach, Maggie wondered if Pike and Tasha might possibly run into each other. Of course, they wouldn't recognize each other. Sitting on the steps of her porch early the next morning she heard the door behind her squeak. Tasha walked from the kitchen with two steaming mugs, each one balanced so not to spill a single drop. She knew her mother could not survive without her coffee fix in the morning Maggie moved over on the steps and Tasha sat down next to her. Each held their cups with both hands, breathing in the steam from the cup as they searched the beach for the morning pelicans.

Knowing the thumping within her chest was not the result of the caffeine that surged through her veins, Maggie's eyes closed. She formed the words in her mind before she spoke. The sudden interruption by Tasha pushed the words back into their hiding places within her mind.

"Mom, there was a guy in the coffee shop; he's a writer. I ran into him the last couple of days. He stays here on the island. He and I had a deep conversation about writing and how trust…"

"Mom, what's wrong"? Tasha stared at her mother, tears were flowing down her cheeks.

"Mom, what is wrong?" Tasha's voice changed from excited to scared.

Without words, Maggie hugged her daughter. Tasha wiped the

tears away from her cheeks as she felt her mother's warm tears on her neck. For a moment, mother and daughter held each other. Only one of them knew the reason for the tears.

Maggie walked into her bedroom and returned with the red box.

"Tasha, I am going finish the story that I started to tell you. This book that you found when you were in college is a part of my life that I did not want to share. It was the most challenging time in my life. I fell in love with that boy in college. He was the one true love of my life.

"I lost him because I was young and scared. We broke up just before graduation, and after we separated I never saw him again. Then I found out that I was pregnant with his child, you.

"The best thing that ever happened to me was you. I got a chance to be a mother and watch you become the strong young woman you are today.

"I think the man you met in the shop is Pike, your father. He does not know he has a daughter. I met him again a few weeks ago and discovered I still had strong feelings for him.

"Tasha, I am so sorry that you never knew your father." Maggie covered her face with her hands and started sobbing, letting go the feelings kept hidden in her heart for decades.

"Mom! I ..." Tasha flashed her anger, partly at her mother and partly at herself. Running out the door, she ran for the beach.

Maggie sat in her rocker on the porch, holding a glass of iced tea. She put the glass to her forehead and felt the coolness. She knew that her eyes were swollen from crying. She also knew that her daughter would be absent for a while.

The storm that had been threatening all day let loose vigorously. It came skating across the Atlantic Ocean. The rain began to pelt the windows of Maggie's cottage. She walked inside and closed the door.

She thought about Tasha and Pike and what would happen when the two met the next time they were in the same place. Maggie wanted to be the one to tell Pike about Tasha.

The words came slowly, they got stuck in Maggie's mouth and seemed to catch on her dry lips. As the words began to mount up, Tasha turned to face her mother. Tasha thought about the box that she had found in her mother's closet so many years ago. As Maggie talked, Tasha reached out and grabbed her mother's hands gently and looked into her eyes. Tasha felt a huge curtain pull away from her eyes. Trivial things began to make sense.

Maggie told Tasha the whole story, of college and being pregnant after college and Pike never knowing. The words began to flow more smoothly as Maggie continued. The story ended as she repeated that the man Tasha had met in the coffee shop was likely Pike, her real father.

"So, he doesn't know?" The words came out with a rush from Tasha. For the first time in the conversation, Maggie looked away from her daughter. Tasha repeated the question. In a voice that Tasha had never heard from her mother the tortured word "No" seemed to void the space between them.

Maggie knew her daughter and knew that she would have to be alone to process for a while. Maggie also knew that Tasha might just run and not look back.

37

It was the smell of fresh brewed coffee that first aroused Maggie from a deep sleep. In fact, it was the best sleep she'd had for a few nights. So many things were circling her mind. Where was Tasha? How could she tell Pike that he had a daughter? The words circling in her head mixing with tears made for sleepless nights alone.

Pulling the covers down and looking at the small clock on the side table by her bed, she blinked not believing that it was nine in the morning. For a morning person, 9:00 a.m. felt like the day was half over. Again, the smell of something else crept into her room. It was cinnamon. Pushing the covers off, she put her feet on the floor pulled on her sweatshirt from off the floor and headed for the kitchen.

Standing in the middle of the kitchen, with white flour covering herself and most everything else was Tasha. Dressed in shorts and a large man's blue T-shirt, Tasha pulled a pan of muffins out of the oven. Turning to the coffee maker, Maggie poured two cups. Tasha smiled as her mother handed her a fresh cup.

With every bit of restraint, Maggie did not ask questions but just waited for the muffins to cool a little before biting into one.

Tasha dusted off the excess flour from her T-shirt grabbed her coffee mug and sat down opposite her mother. Neither woman made eye contact. Each held their mugs; the silence in the room was deafening. Tasha looked up and caught her mother's attention.

"I'm sorry, Mom." This opened a flood gate as the words began to tumble out of Tasha's mouth.

Maggie reached across the table with both hands and gently caressed her daughter's hands. Both mother and daughter sat silently looking at each other as Tasha's words finally stopped. Two coffees and a few muffins later, each had shared their secrets and their regrets with each other. Tasha asked questions about her real father and what happened to him through the years? She wondered what she had missed.

Tasha shared with her mother about Phillip, the man she'd been living with the last four years. She talked about getting pregnant and realizing that she did not want to spend the rest of her life with this man. She shared the pain she felt when she realized that she would have to take care of this baby on her own, which was actually better than spending the rest of her life with him.

Maggie looked at her daughter across the table and remembered when she was her age and the fears and uncertainties about the future—being in love with Pike yet feeling scared when thinking about the rest of her life.

Looking up, she saw Tasha staring at her, tears running down her cheeks.

"Mom, did I make the right choice?" the words were spoken so softly Maggie almost missed them. Taking in the words and watching her daughter, Maggie kept thinking 'What do I know? I'm not even sure of my own life—a life with Pike or life without him?

Maggie put down her coffee, grasped her daughter's hands, looked into her daughter's eyes and spoke words from her heart, hoping they would reach her daughter.

As words spilled out onto the table between them, a picture of Pike started to form in Tasha's mind about her real father. She began to sit back and relax. It was like a huge burden was tumbling off her shoulders. Or perhaps it confirmed some deep feelings that had always existed in some part of her mind about her father.

38

Maggie sat up in bed and looked around her room. Nothing seemed different from yesterday, but overnight her world had changed. Tasha knew who her father was and is. Maggie and Tasha shared tears and broke down some of the walls built over the years. They were beginning to patch and rebuild---the right way.

Today was the day that she was going to tell Pike that he had a daughter. The sun did not show its face this morning. Maggie lay back down in bed and wondered if that was a sign that she should pull the covers up and stay in bed. Maybe today was not a good day to talk with Pike.

Pushing herself up on one elbow she looked outside and whispered aloud, 'At least it isn't raining. With that thought just barely out of her mouth, the crack of thunder broke through. The thunder growled, followed by a low rumbling that shook the walls of the cottage. The thunder followed by the pounding of the rain made it seem as if the thunder and rain were now co-conspirators attacking her cottage. Teaming up, the thunder and rain seemed to be daring her to come outside.

Lifting the corner of her covers Maggie peeked out to see the lightning splash a blinding orb through her bedroom. With all of mother nature screaming at her to stay in bed and avoid the day, she put her feet on the floor and stood. With a shudder that started at her neck and worked its way down her back, she headed to the kitchen hoping that a cup of java would erase the sleep from her mind and jumpstart her heart to face the rigors of the day.

The squeak of the porch screen door jarred her from her thoughts into the present moment. A loud knock at the door completed her journey back into the present. Grabbing a sweatshirt from the floor and a pair of jeans from the white rocker in the corner, she walked from her kitchen to the front porch.

Standing in the shadow of the screen door stood Pike. He was soaking wet, holding two lattes and a soggy bag from the bakery shop. "Maggie!" His voice cut through the roll of thunder which punctuated the moment. Opening the door, Maggie led Pike into the living room. He stood dripping water onto the old hardwood floor. Reaching out to Maggie without a word, he handed her a latte and a soggy bag. She suddenly realized that the rain and the thunder had been preparing her for this moment.

There are some moments that we remember for a lifetime. For Maggie and Pike, it was the moment that they met in the gym at the college dance. Neither of them realized that this moment, although awkward, would be one of many memories they would remind each other of in the coming years.

Maggie went into her bedroom and pulled a blanket off her bed, handed it to Pike, and told him to get out of his wet clothes. A look of surprise appeared on Pike's face but did not last. The first shivers were beginning to work their way through his body. The cold of the fall day accompanied by the rain had changed the course of the conversation between Maggie and Pike on this early morning. As Maggie had suggested, Pike made his way to the bathroom to shed his wet clothes and wrap himself in the blanket that seemed still warm from Maggie's bed. Bundling his clothes, he walked back into the living room and at once smelled the burning logs in the wood-stove and the heat that was removing the chill of the fall rainstorm.

Two old friends and lovers sat facing each other. Words at first were strained and voices tight but this began to lessen. Maggie sat across from Pike in an old sweatshirt from their college days and Pike sat holding his blanket. They listened raptly to each word from the other. Secrets held tightly one from the other slowly made their way out into the space between them.

Pike listened as Maggie talked about the time after they had broken up and gone their separate ways. As trust began to replace pain buried deep in their hearts, they found the person that they knew so many years ago. The heart with many scars can mend and the scars heal through the words of another. Maggie told Pike how she found out she was pregnant after he had left. She talked about trying to find him, but no one knew where he'd gone. After a while she'd given up and moved back into her parent's house.

Maggie had her baby, Tasha, and their life filledl with people. However, something was missing. Sometimes in the early morning hours, she played the what if game. She tried to imagine what he was doing and if he ever thought of her.

Pike sat there watching Maggie with tears running down her cheeks. Reaching out, Pike took Maggie's hand in his and looked at her. She stopped talking and felt Pike looking deeply into her soul. Without shifting or turning away, she looked beyond his eyes and saw something that she recognized from many years in the past.

Pike talked about his life after they split. He talked about the pain and questions that he had and how he just wandered around for a few years, taking jobs here and there. He told her that he had married a few years after they parted. Angie was a woman that he met during a low point in his life. She helped him find his way back. They were married for four years and then the doctor diagnosed her with breast cancer. She lost her battle after two years. Feeling lost again in his life, he returned to school and became a teacher. Giving to others seemed to help him find his way back into life. As with Maggie, there was always something missing in his life.

The writing came later, first as a way of clearing his mind, then as a way of working through his private battles. The surprising part regarding the writings was that people seemed to want to read what he had written. It started with small articles in a local newspaper and then short stories.

The storm that had surrounded them seemed to have dissipated. The thunder faded away and the rain stopped, allowing the words of each to fill the space within the room and within each of them.

The coffee pot emptied and refilled throughout the day. Each had chosen to forgive and begin the process of healing. Pike wanted to know about the girl who was his daughter.

Maggie slowly introduced Pike to the young woman. As Maggie spoke about her daughter, afternoon changed to early evening and the image of the inner Tasha began to form in Pike's mind. With a few little hints from Maggie, he suddenly realized that he had met her in the shop. After all of Pike's questions had been answered, Maggie asked if he wanted to meet her, not as a writer in a coffee shop, but as his daughter?

Pike sat back in his rocker and looked at Maggie. Pike longed to get to know this woman who was his daughter, but he needed some time to process everything he'd heard. Maggie sat back in her rocker and smiled, maybe for the first time all day. As they each sat in their rocker, the back and forth rhythm of the rockers began to mimic their breathing. Eyes closed as each drifted off to sleep.

Sometime much later in the night, the sky threatening, and the storm having long lost its power, words that had been filling the room now seemed to have faded away. The gentle rhythm of their breathing seemed almost choreographed. The fire in the woodstove, having been fed diligently throughout the day, seemed to be going to sleep also.

Maggie awoke first and looked at Pike, his chest rising and falling in its own rhythm, the rocking of the chair long lost to the escape of sleep. Standing, Maggie moved over to Pike and put a blanket over him as he slept. He shifted in the rocker and then fell back into soft breathing. Maggie made her way to the couch with a blue blanket taken from the linen closet. She fell asleep wrapped in her blanket, the burden of all the secrets slipped away.

Sometime in the middle of the night, Pike awoke, stood, stretched his muscles and looked around the room. Maggie was sleeping peacefully on the couch. Pike lifted her legs, then sat down on the couch and put her legs back across his lap. Maggie stirred but did not awaken. Pike leaned back against the couch and fell asleep.

39

Two things reached out and knocked the wind out of Tasha as she entered Maggie's cottage. First was the homey comfort she had rarely felt in her lifetime, and the second was her mother sleeping on the couch with her feet resting in the lap of a man sleeping with her. As she looked more closely at the man, she felt like she'd seen him before. It was the beard that filled in the pieces of the puzzle for her. This was definitely the man from the coffee shop.

It was the sudden realization of this man's possible identity that caused her to drop her mug. It fell to the floor with a splash, but what awakened Maggie and Pike was the scream that Tasha let out as the hot coffee spilled on her feet. They both jumped from dead sleep to full wakefulness in a matter of seconds.

Maggie looked at Pike and realized that her legs were crossing his. The second thing she noticed was that the blanket she had put over Pike was now covering her. It was the last thing, that made everything else so much more important. It was Tasha looking at her mother as she reached down to pick up the empty coffee cup. Her mother's face turned scarlet and the man at the end of the couch scrambled to push Maggie's legs off him, which caused Maggie to fall off the couch and land in a heap on the floor.

Tasha was the first to laugh and then Maggie started to laugh as Pike reached down to help her off the floor. Standing there in front of her daughter Maggie thought she knew what her daughter felt when she was sixteen and her parents walked into their living room to catch Tasha and her high school boyfriend with his hand underneath Tasha's sweater.

Pike stood there looking at the woman standing in front of him, slowly realizing yes, the friendly young lady at the cafe. In her gaze at Pike, Tasha's face reflected recognition at the similarities and longing to know this man fully. Pike turned and went to the kitchen to get some paper towels to clean up the spilled coffee and to escape from the living room. The two women just stared at each other with dancing eyes. Thinking there must be another way out of the cottage he looked toward the back of the kitchen; no such luck.

Making his way back into the living room, Pike stepped lightly between Maggie and her daughter who were talking in hushed tones to each other. As Pike was on his hands and knees sopping up the coffee, he heard Maggie say with a tease in her voice, "Tasha, this is definitely Pike and, I promise, he is your father."

Tasha's eyes were veiled. Pike looked up from his position on the floor and grinned at Tasha.

Rising, Pike looked at the woman standing in front of him, his daughter. He noticed in her some of the things that he had loved in Maggie so many years before and still saw in her. It was her eyes that most caught his attention. Tasha's dark brown eyes were identical to Maggie's eyes. Then she smiled at Pike and immediately won his heart.

In the years to come they would all remember this day, and each would tell whoever was listening their own version of how the morning unfolded. Each person who told the story had a unique perspective and over the years the story grew and changed; however, the central theme of the story never changed.

As time does, weeks passed with Maggie and Pike learning more about each other in the present, and the past seemed to fade into the background. Neither one was the same person that they had been when they were in college. Their personalities were stronger, and they knew who they were. Like all relationships there were difficulties; however, there was always something that kept pulling them toward each other.

They learned to accept each other and who they were today. Tasha felt the strong attraction between her mother and Pike. She also began to let go of her past and accept this new man in her life.

Tasha and Pike slowly began to get to know each other. It was the writing that most blended them together. It was the writing that would eventually create a strong bond between them neither had ever experienced in the past.

40

There were days that Maggie and Tasha would join the regulars in the morning. The air was turning cooler and jeans and sweatshirts had replaced shorts and T-shirts for the morning walks. Some days as they walked, they would see Pike sitting on the old driftwood log either a book in his hand or a pen with his journal in his lap. The difference now was that Pike would look up and wave to the regulars as they went by.

Mr. Bud, a little slower now, still ran up, stopped, and looked up at Pike, waiting for the inevitable scratch behind his ears and something that would magically appear out of Pike's pocket. Mr. Bud would sit patiently waiting until Pike said, "Find it," and then Mr. Bud would sniff each pocket to find his treat.

Other days the regulars spied Pike and Maggie walking, lost in one another in the early morning or in the evening, just before the sun splashed colors, then died in the sky. Tasha stayed with Pike and Maggie as the season began to change. The season was changing for Tasha also, the baby was making itself felt. Tasha walked a little slower as the weeks passed. Pike seemed happier than the others could ever remember. The arrival of the baby would soon become the center of their attention.

THE EPILOGUE

It is two years later, and Pike and Maggie bought the cottage John had rented to Maggie. Tasha returned to Chicago to continue her writing. The baby is two years old and she is a single mom working on finishing her first book.

The regulars still meet to walk the beach, and John and Rachel are still attempting to figure out exactly how permanent their relationship will be. The sea gulls and the pelicans still search for food along the beach. Sometimes Pike and Maggie join the regulars along the beach. The log that was Pike's place to sit and watch the ocean has been replaced with a wooden bench donated by Pike.

Some of the dogs have changed over the two years. Mr. Bud had done his job and brought together Pike and the regulars and brought Maggie back into Pike's life. Now he is gone.

Tasha and her two-year-old son come to visit Maggie and Pike at their cottage. The scars of their yesterdays have faded and new traditions and celebrations have replaced the memories.

Pike still writes but has switched from a novel to a book of poetry. He can be found often on a Friday night at a small coffee shop now named Pike's: Where Friends Meet. On Friday nights, open mic finds Pike and friends either reading poems or talking politics, reading with those gathered around the shop.

A wall of old books donated by locals fill the shelves surrounding a small woodstove that rests on the north wall. People come in, sit and read books from the shelf, and sometimes take a book home with them and return it later.

Maggie's paintings are displayed in the local library and, at a fetching price, some have even found their way to some of the regulars' homes. Visitors to the island sometimes stop by Maggie and Pike's cottage after hearing about her paintings from the regulars.

As Pike sits on his porch rocking, beside him rests a small Brittany puppy named Little Bud. Like his daddy, he's really good at bringing people together.

A SEQUEL TO THE NOVEL FULL CIRCLE
(This new book will be out next summer 2019)

THE STILT HOUSE

The Stilt House is a sequel to the Full Circle. You will meet some new characters and find some of the characters from Full Circle. A new couple moves onto Pelican Island with some new ideas. Jacob and Sara are from Illinois and making a fresh start in their lives. The islanders have some strong opinions about changes.